M000190086

P. Mann

GALLANT

THE CALL OF THE TRAIL

...two horses   two people   one journey

Claire Eckard

MILL CITY PRESS

Mill City Press, Inc.
2301 Lucien Way #415
Maitland, FL 32751
407.339.4217
www.millcitypress.net

© 2021 by Claire Eckard

All rights reserved. No part of this publication may be
reproduced, stored in a retrieval system, or transmitted,
in any form or by any means, electronic, mechanical,
photocopying, recording, or otherwise, without the prior
written permission of the author.

Due to the changing nature of the Internet, if there are any
web addresses, links, or URLs included in this manuscript,
these may have been altered and may no longer be
accessible. The views and opinions shared in this book
belong solely to the author and do not necessarily reflect
those of the publisher. The publisher, therefore, disclaims
responsibility for the views or opinions expressed within
the work.

Paperback ISBN-13: 978-1-6628-2614-6
Ebook ISBN-13: 978-1-6628-2615-3

For Julie,
For all that you are to me.
Love you a hundred miles and back!

"The hooves of the horses!
-Oh! Witching and sweet
Is the music earth steals from the iron-clad feet.
No whisper of lover, no trilling of bird,
Can stir me as hooves of the horses have stirred."

-Will H Ogilve

TABLE OF CONTENTS

PART TWO

PART THREE

LIST OF ILLUSTRATIONS, BY PHYLICIA MANN

Cover Art, Gallant: The Call of the Trail

FOREWORD

The sport of endurance is enjoyed throughout the world. It connects us to the most amazing of creatures, the horse, in a way that is becoming increasingly rare. As endurance riders we get to spend unlimited hours in the saddle on some of the most beautiful and historic trails across America, even throughout the world. The organization that formed in 1973 as the national governing body for this sport is called the American Endurance Ride Conference (AERC.org). AERC provides rules and regulations that standardize the sport. It sanctions over 700 rides nationwide, offers educational opportunities and promotes scientific research, all with the goal of protecting the safety and enjoyment of all involved, but most especially of our wonderful equine partners.

My hope is that if this is a sport you are unfamiliar with, you will go to their website and learn as much as you can from the wealth of information they provide. They can even connect you to a mentor in your area.

This is a book of fiction, and while I have tried to offer a realistic 'feel' for what this sport is about through the experiences of my characters, I have also taken artistic liberty with some of the standard rules of endurance to be able to tell this story. One of these is that a junior rider MUST always ride with a sponsor. My characters do not.

I would also like to emphasize that the motto of AERC is "To Finish is to Win," meaning that racing to win is not the primary goal for many in this sport. Most are riding to challenge themselves and their equines on trails they would never usually get to experience. They are riding to experience the friendships that are formed on the trail, and in ride camp – friendships that can last a lifetime. They are riding despite personal fears and physical limitations, because they have a passion for this sport and for the horses they get to experience it with. One of the most coveted goals is to become a decade team member, where a horse/human partnership has competed together for ten years or more. Longevity is very much respected in this sport.

There are also some incredible Pioneer rides, such as the ones hosted by Dave and Annie Nicholson through the Western Distance Riders Alliance (WDRA). These are held in some of the most scenic areas across the American West and offer an opportunity to spend multiple days in the saddle while enjoying some incredible scenery. A google search can take the reader to information on these, and other organizations that offer information on endurance riding, competitive trail, and ride and tie events, and a list of useful websites is included in the back of this book under Resources.

I hope you enjoy this first book in The Gallant Series. The characters are very near and dear to my heart and I have thoroughly enjoyed bringing them to life. To see updates on the series and to get information on my other books please go to my website at:

www.claireeckardauthor.com

The Western States Trail Museum

A portion of the proceeds from this series are being donated to the Western States Trail Museum to help fund and support a museum dedicated to preserving the legacy of the Western States Trail, home of the iconic Tevis Cup 100 Mile One Day Ride, and Western States Ultra-marathon 100 Mile Endurance Run. The goal of the museum is to preserve and interpret the history and modern-day uses of the Western States Trail, and to cultivate future endurance enthusiasts. Please go to the author website for more information or check out their Facebook page for up-to-date information at www.facebook.com/wstmuseum.

Two Halves of a Broken Mirror

"Mommy says not everyone has a Great-Grandma like you, at least not live ones!" Thomas said.

"Well, that's probably true," Grace replied, looking at the seven-year-old's face turned up toward her. "Not everyone gets to be eighty-six like me!"

Thomas took a seat next to his grandmother, his face deep in thought.

"Can you still see good enough to read?" he asked, trying to wrap his mind around the fact that his great-grandparents were really old, and possibly falling apart a bit.

"If I squint really hard, I can probably make out most of the letters," Grace answered seriously, although her eyes were laughing at the young boy's questions. Thomas hesitated for a moment before saying,

"My brother says you have some special books in your library, but you don't read them very often because they make you sad."

Grace looked down at the small hand in hers. Her grandson's questions taking her mind back to a time when her own hands had been as small as his and she had run them gently over the body of a newborn colt as if he were the most precious thing in the world.

"It's not the books that make me sad, Thomas. They just bring back a lot of memories from a very long time ago about a horse named Gallant, my first great love."

Her hands were still small, but now they were also fragile. The skin was thin "from wear and tear" as Grace put it, and there were dark spots scattered across the surface, with veins that stood out, creating rifts and valleys like a mountain range on a three-dimensional map.

"But I thought Papa was your first great love, Grandma," Thomas said, looking a little worried.

Grace smiled to herself, and then looked at Thomas. He was too young to understand the kind of love she had experienced in her life, but she hoped that one day he would find one just as powerful. Jack was her greatest love of all, although he was always teasing her that he ranked a close second to a certain horse!

Gallant had stolen her heart from the moment he was born. Together they had journeyed thousands of miles; but more than that, their souls had journeyed together. They had been two halves of a broken mirror that could not see themselves clearly unless they were connected. They had travelled from their birthplace in the Valley of Heart's Delight to this place in the clouds, this mountaintop in Scotts Valley, where, in a way, they would always remain a part of each other.

Thomas scampered off the couch, his thoughts switching to other things.

"Can we go and watch the deer?" he asked excitedly, already heading out to the deck. In the evenings small herds of deer would gather in the pasture, happily munching on the buffet of green grass that the horses had just abandoned.

"I'm not sure they'll be out there quite yet, Thomas," Grace said, but she dutifully stood and followed her grandson outside. As she stepped out onto the deck, the fresh mountain air filled her lungs. This was the reason she and Jack had built here, sensing this place would nurture their family, and all the generations that came after.

Unfortunately, the deer had not yet emerged from their cool hiding spot amongst the trees.

"Well, Thomas, no deer yet, as I suspected. Maybe they will come out later, once it's closer to evening." Grace said, ruffling the soft brown hair that was always messy, as if mirroring the scattered thoughts of the head it sprung from.

Disappointed, Thomas ran back inside and climbed onto the couch, returning to his original train of thought.

"So, Grandma, if your eyes are working, can you get the special books out to read to me?" he asked, blue eyes looking up hopefully.

Thomas was distracted by a shuffling noise and the sound of someone clearing their throat as they came from the study on the far side of the living room. A deep, familiar voice said,

"Am I invited to this little gathering, then, Thomas? Or do I have to sit outside with the squirrels while your grandmother reads to you?"

"Papa!" Thomas exclaimed, running over to the man who was entering the room, his twisted fingers wrapped tightly around the book he was carrying. Thomas gave his great-grandfather a warm hug around the legs, then grabbed his free hand and tugged him closer to where Grace sat on the couch.

"Course you're invited!" he said, giggling at the thought of Papa sitting outside on the deck covered in squirrels. "I thought you were still busy in your study!"

Grace looked across the room to her husband of six-ty-four years and smiled. Together, Jack and Grace had raised two sons and a daughter, and now, generations later, their family tree was a sprawling masterpiece with even deeper roots than those of the orchards of pear trees where Grace had grown up.

The book in Jack's hand was a little tattered and torn on the edges, the pages were yellowing with age, and the picture on the cover had faded slightly.

"It seems like reading this to our younger genera-tions has become quite the family tradition!" Jack stated, winking at Grace as he sat down next to her.

"Why is the book so special, Papa?" Thomas said as he snuggled against Grace's side, making himself comfortable.

"This book is special because it's the true story of your grandmother and her first love, a horse named Gallant. Together, they became famous in the sport of endurance riding, some say even legendary!" Jack answered, grinning as the young boy stared at his grandmother, who seemed a lot more impressive all of a sudden.

"You had a horse that was a legend, Grandma?" he asked, his voice tinged with awe.

"Your Grandmother was also quite the legend, Thomas," Jack said, then added in a suspenseful tone, "Gallant had to race against The Almighty Flash, a horse with such darkness in his soul that he was feared by everyone, and challenged by no one! Are you sure you're old enough to sit still and listen to the story carefully?"

Thomas' eyes had grown big and round at the mention of The Almighty Flash! He couldn't wait to hear how Gallant had challenged a horse as scary as that one sounded! He eagerly nodded his agreement. He was pretty sure he could be still for a really long time unless he needed to go to the bathroom. At that thought, he scampered off to take care of business, leaving Grace and Jack alone for a moment.

Jack glanced down at the book in his hands and turned to Grace, looking deeply into her eyes. The look carried the weight of over seven decades.

"If Gallant hadn't chosen me that day, I may never have found you. What would our lives have been like then?" he said seriously, knowing that not a day had gone by where he hadn't been grateful to have Grace by his side.

"Thankfully, we will never know." Grace replied.

As Thomas walked back into the room, the moment was broken, and Jack put on his best grouchy voice. "Now where are those darned reading glasses of mine!"

Thomas giggled, pointing to the end of his grandfather's nose.

"Oh, yes!" Jack said. "There they are. Thank you, Thomas."

And with that, Jack's rich, warm voice resonated through the living room as the young child, three generations removed from his elders, found himself drawn into the story of a horse named Gallant, and the girl who loved him.

PART ONE

Chapter One

THE IMPRINTING WAS DONE

The foal opened his eyes slowly. The stress of being born had left him panting and disoriented, and the strange new world he found himself in was full of unfamiliar sounds and smells. He was laying on a bed of sweet-smelling straw that pricked and irritated the sensitive skin of his newborn body. He felt his lungs expand and relax with each new breath, but he felt panicked and alone until he became aware of a comforting muzzle and the warmth of his mother's breath on his face. She began gently licking and nuzzling this small creature she had just birthed.

The humans that had been drawn from their beds to witness this early morning miracle looked over the stall door, talking in hushed tones, wrapped in blankets with warm mugs of coffee cradled in their hands. They whispered and motioned to each other excitedly at the perfect form of the newborn foal laying at his mother's feet. Magri's heart swelled with pride as she continued cleaning his damp body with her warm tongue. The shared experience of each other's touch and smell

GALLANT

would form an unbreakable bond in those early months.
She would be his anchor in this new world, never letting
him stray too far until he grew strong and independent,
able to move on to new adventures without craving her
reassuring presence.

One of the humans was a tiny figure, a small girl-
child who could barely see over the stall door even if
she stood on the very tips of her toes. She was desperate
to see the new baby creature that had just entered the
world. The child felt the door shift inwards as she leaned
on it to peer over and she took the opportunity to slip
quietly into the birthing space. She had curious blue
eyes and dark hair falling in tendrils around cheeks that
were rosy from the chilly air. She had grown up around
the horses. She recognized their sounds from when she
was in her mother's womb, and as a baby her mother
would often place her stroller in the barn as she did her
chores and the young girl would be lulled to sleep by
the sound of the horses munching on their feed, calling
softly to each other.

However, entering the stall of a new mother with
her foal could be dangerous, and the adults sucked in
a breath of dismay when they realized what she had
done. The child's mother moved toward the opening,
intending to step in and lift her daughter away from
danger, but her sister put a hand on her arm and nodded
in the direction of the foal. The young girl was curled
up into the space alongside the foal's belly and was
humming softly to it, running her small hands up and

2

down the foal's neck while Magri nickered her approval and stood protectively over them both. The foal lay still beneath the child's hands, welcoming the feel of the small body curled against his. He could feel her heartbeat against his own and the vibration of her cheek as she hummed. After the trauma of his birth the foal found comfort in the tiny being, and it helped him adjust to this new world he suddenly found himself a part of.

"I've never seen anything like it," whispered one of the adults to the other.

"Gracie has always been as much horse as human," said Harriet, Gracie's mother. "I'm surprised her first sound as a baby wasn't a neigh!"

Still, the adults knew there was a risk in where the child lay, and the girl's mother crept quietly in to disentangle her daughter from the limbs of the newborn. The foal opened his eyes and looked solemnly at the girl as she was taken away, offering a faint nickering cry. Hers was the first human touch he had felt, and the imprinting was done. He would always recognize her smell, the sound of her voice, and the gentle touch of her hands.

Gracie whimpered at being taken away from the young horse, but the excitement of the night had caught up with her and she was ready to return to her warm bed. Harriet carried her away from the stable, the girl's head resting on her mother's shoulder. She waved a sleepy goodbye to the foal and let her eyes close. That night she would dream of riding him through the orchards in the valley they called home. In her dream the foal had grown tall and strong, and she straddled him bareback, wrapping her legs under his sides and burying her hands in his mane as he flew between the rows of pear trees bathed in the glow of the moonlight.

The foal lay still for a few more moments until the humans left and then began struggling to stand. Instinct told him he needed to rise as soon as possible, that he should not lay on the ground for too long. He managed to push his front legs underneath him and lift his chest for a few seconds before crumpling back down onto the straw. His mother encouraged his efforts by nudging his sides with her muzzle. This time when he tried, he was able to lift his front end and drag his back legs beneath him, straining to straighten them, his body dangling in the air before gravity rudely dragged him down to the straw once again. He kept up his struggles, over and over, until finally all four hooves were on the ground, topped by wobbly legs and a swaying body. He took a few deep breaths, determined to overcome this first obstacle of his new life. Each time he rose he was quicker, smoother, his legs finally understanding what was being asked of them and eventually he stood longer, swaying less, until his body held tall and firm. Once he was balanced, Magri moved her body close to his, guiding him under her belly, knowing he must be thirsty after his efforts. He nudged around, not quite sure what he was searching for until he found it. When he did, he closed his eyes and drank the rich, milky liquid until he was overwhelmed with the need to rest once more. He collapsed back onto the straw, falling immediately into a deep and dreamless sleep.

Chapter Two

WAITING FOR HIM TO SAY THE ACTUAL WORDS

T he next morning Gracie begged her mother to take her back to the barn to see the foal. Now a few hours old, the foal was able to move around precariously on his long legs, even prancing for a few steps as he celebrated his new life and full belly. He was a voracious eater, and Magri was a good mother, standing patiently as the foal nuzzled and poked at her full udder to stimulate the milk. Then he would latch on, wrapping his lips and tongue around the teat, his tail frantically moving back and forth as he drank his fill.

Gracie watched his antics and then asked her mother if Magri and the foal could be let outside into the pasture attached to the birthing stall. The weather had improved in the last few hours, and although still cold, the ground offered a firm footing that would not endanger the young one as he continued to learn how to use his long limbs. Harriet entered the stall and Gracie followed. As her mother went to open the gate to the

paddock, Gracie immediately moved to the foal's side, reaching for him. Initially the foal was startled, until he tentatively reached his muzzle toward her, sniffing at her hand, her clothes, remembering her touch from a few hours previously. Harriet smiled as she turned and saw her small daughter standing so close to the new foal, her hands roaming over his body and her eyes wide with wonder.

"He remembers me, Mother!" Gracie exclaimed. "Look, he lets me touch him all over, even his little ears!"

Harriet watched as the two young lives continued to explore each other for a few more moments. "How about we let the little one outside now, Gracie? Magri will keep a close eye on him so he will be safe, and we will leave the gate to the stall open so they can come inside if it gets too cold, or if he needs to lay down and rest."

Gracie nodded, and then watched as Magri prodded her son in the direction of the opening. At first, he appeared hesitant. The light was bright out there, much brighter than the stall he had become accustomed to. But as his mother moved toward the cold air, he stayed by her side and moved with her. The moment his hooves touched the blades of grass and hardened mud, so different from the soft padding of straw he was used to, he stopped. He sniffed the ground, the grass tickling his nostrils. He pulled back and let out a little snort which made him jump, as he had never heard himself make that sound before. Gracie laughed.

"He's a funny little thing!" her mother exclaimed.

Within a few minutes he was moving confidently around the small paddock, exploring everything within his reach. He moved tentatively toward each new object, reaching out his nose and sniffing cautiously, barely touching it. If it concerned him, he would retreat to his mother's side for reassurance, until a few seconds later curiosity would overcome his fear once again, and he would return with a reinforced bravery. In this manner he explored the fencing, the water tub, the hay rack and the trees, taking in all the sights and smells around him that were a part of his new world.

Just as he was settling down, a large, gangly, German Shepherd puppy came bounding toward the fence where Gracie and her mother stood. He toppled to a halt, all legs and lolling tongue, still young enough to be uncoordinated at rates of speed. He looked up at the humans and then put his front paws up on the first rung of the fence.

"Fling!" Gracie exclaimed. "Don't scare the new baby horse!"

Fling looked up at Gracie, panting. He had run from the farmhouse at a full gallop when Gracie's father, Roy, had let him out, and he was eager to see what all the excitement was about.

Roy approached the group at a slower pace, coffee mug in hand, steam rising from its surface in the cool air of the morning. If this had been a weekday he would have been up and working by now, preparing for the upcoming season of his pear harvest and talking to his buyers about their needs.

Roy was known as a good and fair businessman. His pears were renowned for their high quality, and his orchards produced consistent fruit, thanks to his good management and the dark adobe soil of the valley. Some of his pears were sold at the local stores and farm stands, while others graced the dinner plates in restaurants as far away as London.

Today, however, was Sunday, a day of rest for the family. As Roy joined Harriet and his daughter by the paddock fence, he found it hard not to smile at the new foal as it touched noses with Fling, then jumped backward, toppling off balance as the puppy yelped excitedly.

"Well, I have to say, he's a handsome little fella," said Roy. Gracie seemed to be the only one of his children that had followed in her mother's horse-crazed footsteps. The older children, Bill and Nancy, would rather be playing with the frogs in the creek than be anywhere near the barn, but Gracie had that look of undeniable obsession whenever she was around the horses.

Watching Gracie and the foal, Roy's thoughts wandered to how long it would be before this way of life would change, the verdant soil of this valley becoming the latest surface for a new freeway or shopping mall. He sighed, knowing that sooner or later the inevitable would happen.

Gracie's giggles brought him back to the present. The foal had figured out how to use his gangly legs to run fast, circling the tree and jumping the fallen branches. Magri stood in the middle of the paddock, patiently watching her new son as he ran and bounded back and forth.

Gracie squealed in delight and ran along the fence next to the foal as he flew from one end of the paddock to the other racing the little girl; six long, skinny legs between them going as fast as they could. Gracie, with

her dark hair, and the foal with his dark mane and tail, were well matched in their delight of the morning.

Finally, they both came to a halt, panting from their exertions.

"Did you see how fast he went, Mother! Can you believe how brave he is already? His name should be Gallant! That means brave, you know!" Gracie said excitedly. "He could be my very own horse and I promise I will take care of him every day for his whole life. I really will!"

"That's an awfully big promise to make, Gracie," Harriet pointed out, looking over her daughter's head at Roy and raising her eyebrows at him.

Gracie looked up at her father, her blue eyes wide and pleading.

"Can Gallant be mine, Daddy?" Gracie asked her father, realizing she wanted him to say yes more than anything she had ever wanted before in her whole life.

"When is your birthday, Gracie?" Roy asked in a very serious voice.

"It's today, Daddy! You know that! We're having a party later with a cake and everything! Right, Mother?" Harriet nodded, smiling.

"And when was Gallant born, Gracie?" Roy continued.

"He was born today, Daddy! Very early in the morning. Mother let me watch, and I even got to touch him right after he was born. Gosh, Gallant and I share the same birthday!" Gracie had only just realized this coincidence of the foal's birth.

She looked back and forth between her parents, her lower lip starting to quiver as she realized where this conversation might be going. She crossed her fingers and clenched them against her sides, not taking her eyes off her father's face, waiting for him to say the actual words. Suddenly she felt a wet muzzle nuzzling the back of her dress and turned to see Gallant standing behind her, seeking her attention. He was ready to run and play again.

"It looks like your new foal is going to be rather demanding, Gracie," Roy said finally.

As his words sank in Gracie's eyes filled with tears. "Really, Daddy? Gallant is mine? Oh, thank you, Daddy! Thank you, Mother!"

As Roy nodded, Gracie grabbed his legs in a quick hug before climbing through the slats in the fence and into the paddock with Gallant. She put her tiny arms around the foal's neck and wiped her happy tears into his mane. Gallant nudged against her body but didn't struggle to be free of her grasp. He rested his head in the child's arms. Part of him wanted to go and play, to chase the leaves that fell from the trees, teasing him on their downward journey, but he knew the right thing to do was to stay here for now. If Gracie needed him, he would be there for her, always. From the moment this girl had curled her body against his, comforting him after his birth, he knew that he needed her just as he needed his own mother, it was just meant to be. Magri moved over to stand next to them, rubbing her lips against her son's body, rewarding him for being patient and kind. She wasn't threatened by his love for Gracie. In fact, she seemed to accept Gracie as a member of their little family. Magri loved her offspring fiercely. Between her and Gracie, Gallant would be surrounded by all the love and attention a new life deserved.

*****

Dirk decided to inspect the newborn foals himself this year. He needed a colt who could replace his famous stallion, Baltazar, in a few years. He would keep only the best and get rid of the others. Raising horses was expensive and Dirk was not going to raise any that did not show promise from birth. His plan was to see what the young horses could do on the endurance circuit for a few years, and which showed the most promise. Whichever of his horses placed well in the most iconic endurance race in the world, the Tevis Cup, would become his new breeding stallion.

Kingdom Stables was located in Scottsdale, Arizona, on a prime piece of real estate close to the famous WestWorld, where one of the most prestigious Arabian shows was held each Spring. While Dirk often entered his youngsters in the halter classes, his primary focus was on breeding the best endurance horses in the world, and Kingdom stables was renowned worldwide for their fine Arabian horseflesh. They demanded high prices from overseas buyers for their endurance stock, and even more for the mares who would continue to produce their famous offspring.

The stable's reputation in the United States was far from exemplary, however. Dirk was known not only as an ambitious and driven man, but one who pushed his horses well beyond their capabilities, race after race, testing their bodies and minds to the limits to see who would break down, and who would survive. The ones that broke down were never seen again. Dirk often had his barn manager, Logan, ride his horses in endurance races so if anything went wrong, Dirk could blame the rider and remain an arm's length from any disaster on the trail.

Dirk walked down the breezeway carrying a long riding crop, his large strides those of a confident and determined man. He carried a dressage whip in his hand, which he used often to drive home a point on horses and people alike. He was here to cull the weak.

When he came to the birthing stalls Logan informed him that four foals had been born the night before, but one of the mare's had not survived.

"Show me the foals," Dirk demanded.

The first two stalls contained fillies, both strong and nursing at their mother's teats. They were already steady on their feet and would make fine broodmares in a few years. Dirk continued to the next stall. A small, black colt lay on his side, his mother standing over him protectively. As Dirk rapped on the stall door with his crop the foal barely lifted his head from the straw. He whinnied pitifully. Dirk's eyes narrowed.

"How old is this one?" Dirk snapped at Logan, who flinched at the question.

"He's five hours old, Sir. Born about two in the morning. He has suckled a couple of times since then. Sometimes they're just slow starters, Sir."

"I asked for information, not your opinion," Dirk replied impatiently, his eye's narrowing to slits as he looked Logan up and down.

"Show me the last one." He snapped.

In the final stall a bay foal stood over the dead body of the mare who had birthed him. When Dirk rapped on the stall door the colt looked at the man defiantly. Dirk entered the stall and poked his crop against the bloated belly of the mare. The foal stood his ground.

"How old is he?" Dirk asked, not taking his eyes off the foal.

"The mare's been dead for six hours," Logan replied. "The foal hasn't eaten, and he hasn't laid down since he figured out how to stand."

Dirk looked at the foal and saw the challenge in his eyes. This one was a fighter. With no sustenance he was surviving on willpower alone. Dirk left the stall, glancing back at Logan.

"You know what to do," he said.

Logan's face reddened in anger, but he couldn't afford to lose his job, even one as unsavory as this one. He had a family to feed at home and rent to pay. He looked down at his feet. "Yes, sir," he muttered.

*****

Flash remembered leaving a warm place and falling onto something prickly. It was suddenly cold, and his eyes were straining to make sense of shadow and light. He heard sounds—deep, guttural, angry voices. He felt the heaving warmth of a body next to him that twitched and moved. He struggled, and a slimy, thin membrane fell off him, the cold air even more apparent now against his steaming wet body. His lungs filled, the breath burning his insides, his nostrils gurgling with fluid from the birthing process. He rested for a moment, then struggled, gasping at the effort to rise. He fell against the body that lay next to him, smelling a metallic sharpness in the air. He struggled again and managed to rise, stagger a few steps, and fell again. He found himself staring into his mother's face. The eyes staring back were glazed with shadow and regret. Her breaths were staggered, wheezing, coming in great gasps followed by shallow gulps. She tried to move her head, to look at him, her eyes begging him to come closer.

"My son," he heard her say. "Listen carefully to me as I will not be here to raise you." She paused, fighting against the pain it took to speak. "You must stand as soon as you can and stay standing for as long as you can bear it. You must be brave and not let the humans intim-idate you. The mean one hates weakness of any kind."

Her breaths were shallow now, and the foal had to reach closer toward her muzzle to hear what she was saying, "Find the moon liquid and drink as much as you can, wherever you can find it. Fill your belly. When you are able, take every chance to run, as far and as fast as you can. You need to become strong because they will prey on the weak." Her eyes started to close as she des-perately tried to stay with him.

The foal stared at the face before him, taking in every hair, every marking, feeling every ounce of the struggle she made to stay alive for just one more moment. "Are you my mother?" he asked.

"You have no mother," she said sharply, the words costing her dearly. "You have only yourself. You are The Almighty Flash, and you must live up to the name I have given you." Her eyes opened then and drank in the sight of him before the merciful darkness came, her final breath washing over him. He tried to capture it and draw it into his own lungs, flooding every cell with all he had left of her being.

Flash stared at her for many seconds before rising off the ground once more. He stood over her, remem-bering her words. Hers would be the voice he would hear in his darkest moments. He would crave the love that might have been between them, while shutting out that emotion from all who came after her. He would have no one to rely on in this life except himself and he must do whatever it took to survive. He stood there for hours as her body cooled and stiffened. He shivered with cold and exhaustion but still he did not lay down. "Weakness is my enemy," he repeated to himself. "I must stay strong."

A beast that stood on two legs entered his stall and stared him directly in the eye. The foal did not back away, and he did not back down. After he left, the others came in and took him away from the body of his mother. They draped him in a black coat that smelled of blood and warm flesh and shoved him under the belly of a stranger. She was upset, shaking, as if she had lost something precious, but as her muzzle sniffed at the strange coat he was wearing, she calmed and accepted the new young one.

Find the moon liquid and drink as much as you can, his mother had said, and he did as she had bid him, a treasure stolen from the one who had not been given the chance to live. The foal drank and drank, only stopping when he could drink no more. Only then did he lay down and rest, knowing that every day would be a fight, and he needed to be strong for it.

I have no mother, he thought as his eyelids grew heavy. I have only myself. This is the life I have been given.

Chapter Three

OF WOOD AND WIRE

A s Gracie grew her world changed. School became part of her day. Her life became more structured, and she had to learn how to navigate a different world of homework and expectations. Most of the children in her school were unfamiliar with the kind of rural life she lived, and some would tease her because of it, calling her the farmer's daughter. She took the teasing in the good-natured way it was intended, her mind usually distracted with wondering what Gallant was doing at that very moment back at home. As the youngest of three children and living so far out in the country, Gallant and Fling had become her friends, her playmates, and her confidants. She was happy so long as she was at home with her animals surrounding her.

Gracie and Gallant grew quickly over the following months and years. Their legs grew longer, sturdier, stronger. They both ran faster and grew braver in their explorations. They became less dependent on those around them, even as they gravitated more toward each other. When Gracie was not at school, or doing her chores or homework, she and Gallant were usually together. Gallant and Fling learned to listen for the sound of the school bus stopping at the end of the long dirt road that led to the stables, and they would try to outrace each other to see who could get to Gracie first. She would climb down out of the bus, backpack bouncing on her back and lunchbox swinging by her side. After greeting Fling, she would look for Gallant who would be waiting for her at the end of his paddock, neighing his familiar welcome. Gallant would then trot alongside her and Fling as they made their way down the long driveway, and every day she would blow him a kiss before turning toward the house, promising to come see him once she had done her homework and chores.

Seeds of magic had been planted the night that Gallant was born, and as Gracie grew up alongside the foal their friendship solidified and strengthened. At first Gracie was not allowed to take him from the paddock, but as she grew older and stronger, and the adults witnessed the great care Gallant took around her, it became a common sight to see her wandering around the ranch leading her horse, proudly decked out in a bright red halter and lead rope, a gift for Gracie's eighth birthday, and Gallants third. Gallant was always just a step behind Gracie, shadowing her every move. He knew that when she came into the barn with the red halter in her hand, he would get to explore the ranch and spend time with his favorite person. She would come into his stall, and he would lower his head so she could slip the halter easily over his nose and ears. Then she would whisper to him, "You are the best horse in the whole world" as her face nestled into his dark mane, fingers circling his locks into tangled masses that she would have to comb out later. To her, Gallant was the most incredible horse she had ever seen. If he had any flaws, her loving eyes would never see them.

Gallant would never get tired of their time together. To him, her voice was as sweet as the carrots she would bring him to munch on while they had their conversations. Her siblings were always too busy getting through their own day to talk to their little sister, but Gallant always offered a willing ear and a comforting neck for Gracie to wrap her arms around.

On the weekends, Harriet came out to the barn with Gracie, and they would tie Gallant and Magri next to each other at the hitching post and groom them. Side by side, the grey mare and her bay son seemed so different, and yet one would not have come into this world without the other. At three years old, the crooked white blaze on Gallant's face was striking against the deep bay of his coat. He was an average size for his age, still gawky in his growing body.

"How big do you think Gallant will get, Mother?" Gracie asked.

"Arabians are often slow to mature, Gracie. I think he might end up at around fifteen hands."

Gracie adored her mother, and she treasured these moments they shared with the horses, so she tried to drag them out for as long as she could.

"Am I brushing him the right way, Mother?" Gracie would ask, as if she hadn't spent three years grooming her horse already.

"Long, steady strokes, Gracie. Brush in the direction his coat is going, not against it. Not too hard, and not too soft. There, that's right. Good girl."

"I expect Gallant is going to be really fast, don't you think, Mother?"

"Judging by the way he runs around his paddock I think you are right!"

And they would continue on, the horses resting peacefully side by side, hips cocked, and eyes closed as they enjoyed the brushing.

Although Gallant loved growing up in the Valley of Heart's Delight, he wondered when all the exciting adventures Gracie often talked about would begin. He didn't know what any other kind of life would look like, but sometimes in his paddock he would start running, and he didn't want to stop. He would look out at the hills and wonder what it would be like if they would open the gate to his paddock and let him run into the wide, open space. He felt the call of the trail, and he wanted to run as far and as fast as he could, the wind lifting his mane and the smells taunting his nostrils. Gallant didn't know what might be out there in the world for him, but as he got older, he knew he was missing something, and it felt like he was being left behind in some way.

One day a small black and white pony arrived at the stables. His name was Andy. Harriet bought him so Gracie would have something small and safe to ride. Now, when the horses were taken out to be groomed, Andy was included. This wouldn't have been so bad, other than once the grooming was done, Gallant was now put back in his paddock while Gracie and Harriet took Andy and Magri out for a ride.

Gallant experienced jealousy for the first time in his life. He was jealous of the time Gracie spent with Andy, and jealous that Andy got to go out into the hills that he so desperately craved to run across. One day, as Gallant watched Gracie tack Andy up and take him out to the stable yard with her mother and Magri, his jealousy changed to anger. Harriet and Gracie mounted and left the stable area at a walk, heading out to the entrance of the trail that would lead them into the hills flanking the north side of the ranch. Gallant could see them from his paddock, and he called repeatedly to Gracie as he ran the fence line, up and back, up and back, frustrated that he was stuck there and unable to join in any of the fun. He began circling his paddock faster and faster, putting his head down and lifting his tail behind him, trying to run off all his exasperation and anger. He couldn't bear to be there while that stupid little pony got to be with Gracie exploring all the hills and hidden valleys that Gallant had never seen. Without thinking, Gallant began blindly galloping toward the fence. He wanted to be on the other side of it, running free, not contained by wood and wire. As he got closer to the thing that was trapping him, his anger soared, and so did he. His front legs lifted off the ground, and his powerful hind end pushed him upwards until he was flying over the top of the fence, clearing it easily. His front legs dropped to the ground, followed by his hinds, and he was free! He was out in the stable yard all by himself. How had he done that? He could hardly remember! He only knew he couldn't stand being in the paddock any longer! Gallant took off at a canter, thrilled to explore the trails he knew were out there waiting for him.

*****

Harriet and Gracie had been riding for thirty minutes when they heard the pounding of hooves behind them.

"Gallant!" Gracie exclaimed. "How did you get out of your paddock?"

Gallant pulled up alongside the pair of riders, proud that he had found them at last, his adrenaline high from the freedom of galloping across the hillside.

"I guess we'll have to cut our ride short and take him back to the ranch," Harriet said. "What a troublemaker! If he's learned how to jump out of his paddock, we're going to have a problem, Gracie."

"Let's just continue on with our ride, Mother. I think he will follow us. He doesn't mean to be any trouble; he just doesn't like getting left behind. Can we keep going and see what he does for a little while? If he misbehaves we can turn back, I promise!"

Gallant was very pleased with himself as Gracie and her mother continued down the trail. He trotted behind them, occasionally moving alongside Gracie and Andy, the pony giving him a look of disdain as he did so.

"I can't believe you had to come and cut in on my time with Gracie," Andy complained to Gallant. "You don't belong out on the trails with us. You're just a baby who belongs in the barnyard!"

"Well, you'd better get used to this, Weasel," Gallant replied. "Because I don't intend to be fenced in any longer. This is too much fun!"

When they slowed to a walk Gallant occasionally stopped to grab a bite of grass, trotting to catch up once the others got a few paces ahead. Gracie looked over and smiled. She was obviously enjoying having him out on the ride with her. Gallant moved closer to Andy's side so Gracie could reach over and stroke his neck.

"Get off my flank, Gallant," Andy demanded. "Get back behind me where you belong!"

"I belong right here, by Gracie's side," Gallant responded. "I always have, and I always will!"

Gracie was in Heaven. She couldn't believe she was on her favorite trail with Gallant following along.

"He's being really good, isn't he Mother!" she called ahead to Harriet. "Can we bring him along from now on? He's old enough to need more exercise, anyway, isn't he?"

"Let's see how he does for the rest of the ride, Gracie," Harriet called back. "So far he's doing really well though. I think you're right. He just didn't like being left behind at the stables."

When they returned to the ranch an hour later, Gallant followed them quietly over to the hitching post and stood there next to the other horses as if he were tied to it like they were. Gracie looked at her mother and they both broke into laughter at the sight.

"Well, I guess that seals the deal," Harriet said. "Gallant can follow us out next time, but you can actually open the gate to let him out, Gracie, rather than him jumping it!"

Gracie brushed Andy and put him away in his stall, and then did the same with Gallant, whispering to him, "One day it will be you and me, Gallant. I just need to practice riding on Andy so that I can ride you when you're ready! Otherwise, neither of us will know what we're doing!"

The next time Andy and Gallant were tied up next to each other being groomed, Andy began teasing Gallant, saying. "One of us is not getting ridden today, and I know who!"

Gallant stomped his feet and snapped back, "One of us isn't getting any taller, and I know who!"

Magri interjected before the taunting got worse. "Stop it, you two! I'm trying to relax and enjoy my brushing but it's hard with all your squabbling!" Then she whispered quietly to Gallant so that Andy couldn't hear, "Children outgrow ponies quickly, Gallant. Be nice to Andy because he probably has to move to a new home every few years, while you will get to live here with Gracie forever."

When his mother said that Gallant felt bad for being jealous of Andy and decided he would try to make friends with the pony, even if he was obnoxious.

*****

Before long, Gracie began to crave the freedom of riding more and more and began sneaking out at night to hop on the pony bareback and ride down the rows of pear trees in the moonlight, always accompanied by her faithful Fling. The second step going down the stairs from her bedroom squeaked terribly, so she devised an escape route by climbing off her balcony onto the adjacent attic roof. From there she would drop down onto the garage, and then climb down to the ground.

"Come on, Fling," she would whisper as she opened the front door to let him out. Girl and dog would run across the yard from the house to the barn, Gracie always giving Gallant a quick kiss on his sleepy muzzle before grabbing Andy from the adjoining stall.

Andy was not the most cooperative pony, and Gracie had to mount him quickly by swinging herself over the pony's back and then throwing her leg over before he took off without her. Gracie would then point him in the direction of the orchards, sometimes well-lit in the moonlight, other times dark and mysterious. She needed to keep her wits about her as Andy would try to knock her off his back by running under the low hanging branches of the pear trees. Gracie learned to grab an overhead branch and pull herself out of the saddle, dropping quickly to the ground rather than risk being knocked off, unable to control her fall. But riding through the orchards at night made all his shenanigans worth putting up with. The sensation of riding him made the whole world disappear as Gracie became mesmerized by the sway and smell of the pony she straddled. She felt like she and Andy were the only ones hurtling through the deep stillness of the universe. It was magical.

Gallant was confused. He didn't know why he was not being ridden and taken on adventures. He was far bigger than Andy, and he was getting restless that he didn't seem to have any particular job to do, other than being Gracie's companion. Magri's foals were usually sent away to the trainer at the age of three. They were taught how to accept the weight of a saddle and a rider, and how to respond to the feel of the bit in their mouths, connected to the riders' hands by the reins. They learned how to move away from the pressure of the riders' leg, recognizing the cues so that rider and horse could move safely as one unit. Harriet had hesitated to send Gallant away, knowing how heartbroken Gracie would be not having him there. He was tired of being known as the baby, and while running loose on the trails was wonderful, Gallant was beginning to wonder when all these adventures would actually begin. He was restless for more.

*****

Flash was the largest of the colts in the stables. He had taken his mother's advice and always ate and drank as much as he could, taking every opportunity to exercise. While the other horses ran around the paddocks in play, Flash counted the laps he did around the inside of the fence line, each week striving for more laps, more speed. His mind was focused even at an early age.

At three years old his official training began. There was an exercise machine that moved the horses around in circles, switching direction every three minutes. Several of the colts were run at once, each in their own compartment, and their lungs and legs were built up before they ever felt the weight of a rider on their back. The horses were handled by the workers at the stables, never receiving more than the basics. They were haltered, groomed and had their hooves trimmed and shaped by the farrier. There was no love, no compassion, no relationship at all between human and horse. The twenty foals born the same spring as Flash were soon whittled down to twelve, and then eight. There was no point forming friendships as overnight foals could disappear, the others never knowing where they went.

Flash became a machine, just like the exerciser he was put into.

Often Baltazar was led past on his way to the breeding barn. He held his head and tail high, and pranced lightly on all four legs, his neck arched as his long mane flowed around it. Flash looked at his father as he walked by, admiring him and all he stood for. He had a special stall and paddock all to himself. He received the best feed and care, was groomed meticulously every day, and was paraded in front of all the prospective buyers who came to the stables, showing them the superior genetics of the horses they were looking to purchase. Baltazar was the king of all the horses there, and never paid any attention to his offspring. He had one job in this life, and he was good at it, but that is where his efforts ended.

One morning Flash called to the stallion as he went by, "Father, I am growing big and strong so I can be just like you! I will be the most famous endurance horse in the whole world and will make you proud!"

Baltazar turned his head, looking Flash in the eye. He glanced over his son's frame, noting his height, his musculature, and the confident way he moved compared to the other colts, and he knew then that he may be looking at his replacement. "You have a long way to go, boy." he sneered. "There are many opportunities for failure along the way and I'm sure you will find them. The sooner you realize your life is worthless the less disappointed you will be. Never speak to me again."

Flash narrowed his eyes at the stallion and pinned his ears against his head, lashing out against the pain of the rejection, "Don't worry, Father. The next time I bother talking to you will be the day I take your place and kick you out of here. You will become dog meat while I will take all your mares and be the new king. Never speak to *me* again, and never forget that The Almighty Flash is coming for you!"

His mother had been right. He was alone in this world and could only rely on himself. He put his head down and put even more power into his walk, breathing deeply to fill and expand his lungs. He would never look for approval from anyone again. He would never set himself up for the pain of rejection and he would work every minute of every day to become the best.

He couldn't wait to get out on the trails and prove his superiority to all who raced against him. He would do whatever it took to crush his competition until he had no competition left. He would stand at the starting line of the Tevis Cup and dominate the trail for the win, *and* he would take home the coveted Haggin Cup.

Nothing and no one would stop him.

Chapter Four

A TINY CLOUD OF DUST

G racie shared the same birthday as the Queen of England, so every year, on the morning of her birthday, Gracie would lay in bed imagining what it would be like to spend her special day in England with Her Majesty. She imagined riding Gallant in the Queen's birthday parade through the streets of London, and then taking the Queen to one of the fancy London restaurants that served her father's pears. She thought the Queen might like that. Based on this fact, she fully expected to one day receive a summons for her and Gallant to join Her Majesty at Buckingham Palace.

Each year Gracie was slightly disappointed when the invitation failed to appear, but she remained optimistic. She realized that the Queen was probably waiting for her and Gallant to be old enough to fly to England unaccompanied for their visit. On the morning of her tenth birthday, Gracie awoke with a sense of urgency that the visit with the Queen was surely imminent. Therefore, today was the day that Gallant must learn to be ridden!

Gracie was excited to begin Gallant's training and felt it appropriate that they begin on both of their birthdays. While her siblings were hunting frogs in the creek that ran behind the house, and her parents were waiting in the study for Gracie's aunts and cousins to arrive for the birthday celebrations, Gracie made her way to the stables. Gallant cantered lazily along the fence line of his paddock, arriving at the barn the same time as Gracie. He whinnied excitedly when he saw the red halter in her hands.

"Hey, Gallant," Gracie greeted him.

She entered his stall, and he came right up to her, nuzzling her hand, searching for the piece of carrot he would inevitably find there.

"Happy Birthday, Gallant!" she said. Gallant munched away, looking at her with thoughtful eyes as he always did when she conversed with him.

Gracie slipped the halter over his nose and ears and led him outside to the hitching post where she loosely tied him up. Gracie's hands were strong and efficient, and he enjoyed the feeling of the brush running along his neck and sides, down his back and each leg. Once his body was smooth and shiny, she got the softer brush and groomed his face and forehead. Gallant dropped his head to make it easier for her, his eyes closing in a moment of bliss as she brushed his cheeks and forehead. Since this was a special day, Gracie got out the mane comb, combing out his mane and tail until they looked perfect and flowed around him with the slightest movement.

"There," Gracie said, taking a step back to look at him. "You look more handsome than ever! Let's begin!"

She led him toward the mounting block a few feet away from the hitching post. Despite this being his first official lesson, Gracie was confident that Gallant would calmly do whatever she asked of him. She had no reason to believe otherwise.

"The first thing you must understand is that I'm going to be sitting on your back a lot from now on, and not just leading you around like a baby, or letting you run loose like a dog!" Gracie quipped.

Gallant had no idea what she was telling him, but he was used to the sound of her voice and the feel of her hands. He was not afraid, just curious to see what would happen next.

"Stand here!" Gracie said as she led him alongside the mounting block. She threw the lead rope over his neck and confidently climbed the two steps where she could now see above his back. Gracie had already changed into her best Sunday dress for her birthday party, with her favorite pair of black patent shoes. Her hair was curled and bobbed around her shoulders, which, of course, meant that Gracie could not wear her riding helmet and ruin her beautiful hairstyle before the party. She was sure that by the time her cousins arrived she would be showing them how well Gallant could be ridden. Maybe her father would even take a birthday photograph of her all dressed up, sitting on Gallant's back!

Because Gracie was so confident that Gallant trusted her, she didn't even think to give him any warning of what she was about to do. Gracie had to put more effort into mounting him than her shorter pony. She swung her leg over his rump, landing on his back a little too hard, and she gripped her legs tightly around his middle so she wouldn't fall off, just like she did with Andy.

Gallant had been standing there almost asleep, expecting Gracie to start braiding his mane or weaving wildflowers into it like she usually did. Suddenly, he saw something swinging into the air behind him and he felt a weight landing on his back. He had no idea what it was. He had never felt weight there before and it was a shock to him. Something gripped hard against his sides and he instinctively jumped forward in surprise. *What's going on?* he thought. As quickly as he had felt the weight land on his back it disappeared. At the same time, he heard a scream and saw Gracie fall to the ground beside him, sending up a tiny cloud of dust as she landed with a heavy thud.

The sound scared Gallant and he ran away for a few steps before turning back to see what was going on. Gracie lay in the dirt near the mounting block not making a sound. Gallant moved toward her, nuzzling her gently with his muzzle. Was she sleeping? Sometimes the little girl would come into his stall in the evening and lay down next to him in the straw, and after chatting and murmuring for a while she would become still, her breath even and rhythmic, and they would lay together quietly until her mother came out to take her back to the ranch house. This felt different. There was something red running out of a crack on her chin and mingling with the dirt beneath her head. It smelled funny. He nickered softly to her, hoping she would stir and reach out for him, but nothing happened. Gallant wasn't sure how long he stood there at her side, waiting for her to awaken.

He heard footsteps running toward them, anxious voices calling Gracie's name. Her father arrived first, followed by her mother and her siblings. Her aunt, uncle, and cousins were not far behind. Roy pushed Gallant out of the way and knelt by his daughter, his eyes scanning her body to see if there were any obvious injuries other than the cut on her chin. Gracie's right ankle was twisted, her foot splayed at an odd angle.

"Is Gracie going to be alright, Daddy?" Nancy asked anxiously. It scared her to see her baby sister laying there injured. Bill put his arm around her shoulders.

As Gracie came to, she heard one of her cousins snickering and saying to the other, "Look! You can see her underpants!" This comment was met with a sharp reprimand. Gracie's mother hurriedly put Gallant back in his stall, and her father scooped her up, carrying her back to the ranch house. Her right ankle felt funny and hurt a lot, but not as much as her pride as she realized her underpants were probably still showing.

Finding himself in his stall alone, Gallant stood there, confused and shaken. He knew he must have done something terribly wrong. What would happen to him now? He whinnied for his mother, Magri. It was the first time he had needed her in a while, but she was busy in another paddock nursing her latest foal and had not witnessed what had happened. Gallant felt scared. He thought they might send him away for being bad and hurting Gracie, and he would never get to see her, or his mother, again.

A loud vehicle with flashing lights pulled into the driveway by the ranch house, and Gracie was carried out on a flat board and loaded into the back of it. Gallant could hear her crying, and he whinnied loudly for her, letting her know he was sorry, that he hadn't meant to hurt her. He didn't know where they were taking her, only that her parents followed the strange truck in their car, ignoring his calls.

Gracie's aunt fed all the horses that evening, making sure they had plenty of hay and water and were settled for the night, a subdued Fling hovering by her heels the whole time. She looked sadly at Gallant before shaking her head and going back indoors. He stood there in the stall for hours, not eating or drinking. The lead rope weighed down his fancy red halter and dragged on the floor. He fell into a fitful sleep, not waking until early in the morning when he heard the sound of strange voices, and hurried footsteps approaching.

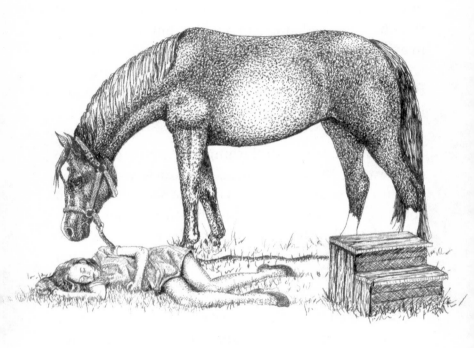

*****

Flash had done well in his training. So well, in fact, that all the other five-year-old colts had been gelded except for Flash and one other, Steel. Each of them had won some local endurance races and both had what Dirk was looking for, a drive to win, combined with natural talent and breeding. Since the Arizona summers were too hot for serious endurance training, Dirk had decreed that each horse would now be sent out to a different barn to take their training to the next level. Steel was sent to Colorado to La Veta Endurance and Racing Stables to train at elevation in the mountains, while Flash was going to the West Coast to train at Greenhill Stables in the foothills of the Sierra's, close to the famous Western States One-hundred-mile Trail where the Tevis Cup race was held every year. Flash knew this decision put him in the number one spot as the future Lead Stallion for Kingdom Stables, with Steel as the backup. The job of Lead Stallion was his to lose.

Flash was transferred to Greenhill Stables for his six-month training program and greeted by Jenny, the trainer, Albert, the groom, and two of the stall cleaners and maintenance men, Larry and Ted. As he was led down the ramp of the trailer, he looked each of the humans over. They would be his servants for the next six months, each there to serve a purpose along his journey. He knew he looked impressive as he walked out into the daylight, his coat gleaming and his muscles rippling with power as he moved. He walked with the authority of a king meeting his subjects for the first time.

As a stallion he could not be stalled next to any mares, so Flash was put in a pen at the end of the row with a large turn-out paddock attached. The stall next to his was empty but would be filled with a gelding, no doubt. There was a pretty little chestnut filly on the far side of the empty pen who watched Flash as he approached. Flash was used to the adoration of mares by now. He expected it.

He was left to settle in for the remainder of the day, even though he was anxious to get on with his training. He knew that here he would be challenged by mountain trails with gullies and ridges, rocky crags and streams and he would have to use his power wisely and learn how to be sure-footed on these technical trails.

He looked around the barn at the other horses who had come from all over the country to be trained there. They all looked like children in a play yard to him; first graders there to learn the basics, while he was there to graduate college. *What a load of useless beasts*, he thought, looking around. They had probably been babied their whole lives and had bought into a life that depended on the emotional support of their human owners. Flash was proud that he had made it on his own, relying on no one but himself, just like he had been told to do by his dying mother. He used the humans to meet his basic needs, but beyond that, he had no use for them. He scraped his foot on the floor of his stall, frustrated to be standing there when he should be out on the trails adding the next layer to his fitness training. He didn't care what Steel was doing in Colorado. No horse would be a threat to him once he finished here. His plans were falling into place, bit by bit, and there was no question in Flash's mind that he was the next king.

Chapter Five

I THINK THAT MAYBE I DID A TERRIBLE THING

The truck pulled up close to Gallant's stall and two men got out. There was a horse trailer hooked up to the back of the truck and the men went around and opened the door at the rear of it. They lowered a ramp and then one of them began walking toward Gallant's stall. Gallant lifted his head quickly as the man approached. He looked warily at the stranger. He had never seen him before and had no idea who he was or what he was doing there. The man opened the stall door and approached him. Gallant instinctively moved away, his ears pricked up in fear, his breath snorting through his nostrils. The door to the paddock was still closed so he only had a small space to try and escape. He ran back and forth along the back wall, the man jumping in front of him, forcing him into the back corner where he lunged out and grabbed the lead rope still hanging from his halter. The hands at the end of the rope felt different than Gracie's. Hers were soft and gentle, the mans were strong and rough.

"Hold still, you little brat!" he snarled, yanking on the halter. In the adjoining stall, Magri started lunging against the wall that separated them, her ears pinned back in anger, even as she tried to offer comfort to her son.

Once the man had the rope, Gallant knew he would not be able to get away.

"What's happening, Mother?" he called frantically. "I can't get away. He won't let go of the rope!"

Gallant tried to pull backward but lost his footing in the struggle. Feeling exhausted and defeated, he stood there shaking, eyes fixed on the stranger. The man dragged him out of the stall.

"Mother!" he screamed, "Where are they taking me?"

Magri was helpless. She couldn't get out of her stall to help him. She called out to him, over and over, "I love you, Gallant! Be brave! I love you, my son!"

The man led the still struggling Gallant toward the back of the horse trailer where the second man stood waiting.

"He's a strong one," the first man said.

"Small but scrappy. He could give us some trouble. Better get the whip out in case he needs some encouragement getting in."

The second man opened a side door of the trailer and emerged holding something that looked like a long stick with a skinny rope at the end. As the first man led Gallant to the trailer, the second man waved the stick behind him, forcing Gallant to jump forward. The inside of the trailer looked dark and scary and was nothing like the comfort of his stall. The roof was very low, and the space was tight. Gallant tried to back down the ramp. He didn't want to stay in there! The second man narrowed his eyes, his patience wearing thin. He raised his arm and angrily brought the whip down, striking Gallant twice on the sensitive area above his hocks. Gallant panicked at the unexpected sting on his back legs and ran forward into the trailer once again. It all happened so fast, and now he found himself trapped. The ramp was lifted, and the door closed behind him.

Gallant had never known fear at the hands of humans. He had always been cared for with love and respect. He had never been handled roughly or made to do something that scared him. Now he was trapped inside this steel box and the truck was beginning to move, carrying him away from all he knew and loved! He could hear his mother screaming his name. He called to her through the small window, desperate pleas for help, and listened to her answering calls grow fainter as the truck kept moving, taking him farther and farther away.

The ranch house was getting smaller. As they passed beyond the rows of pear trees, Gallant found himself in a world he knew nothing about, where everything he saw and heard was unfamiliar and strange. There were so many cars rushing by, and huge noisy trucks that seemed so close he cowered away from them in terror. The scenery was forever changing. The orchards faded into the distance, and instead he saw open fields with rolling hills hovering behind them. Layered behind the hills were mountain peaks disappearing into the sky. The earth appeared yellow and parched from lack of rain, the only signs of greenery were the oak trees scattered haphazardly across the landscape. Gallant gazed out the little window wondering where in the world he was being taken.

A few hours later, as he was beginning to get extremely hungry and thirsty, the truck finally slowed down, made a tight right turn, and passed through some large iron gates. The scenery had changed again in the last part of the journey. The countryside had become green and lush, trees clustered together in large groups, and there were ranches everywhere, fence lines butting up against each other, elbowing each other for more space. The road had wound slowly up into the hills he had seen from a distance. The air was chillier, and Gallant shivered, either from cold or anticipation, he was not sure which. Through his little window he could see a lot of open space on the property with trails extending into the foothills, as well as some paddocks with shelters, and shade trees that lined the driveway they were travelling along. The air smelled different, and the horses he could see running along the fence lines of the paddocks all whinnied at the trailer, wondering who was inside. The truck continued to wind its way along the driveway before finally pulling up next to a large barn.

The back door of the trailer opened and light flooded in as the ramp was lowered. There was a woman standing there with the men now. She slowly entered the trailer, reaching for the lead rope that dragged through the shavings at Gallant's feet. He cowered in the corner, still shaking from his experience earlier. The woman had a softer touch than the men, and kinder eyes. She spoke gently to him, and he allowed her to inch closer until her hand rested upon his neck, reassuring him.

"Easy now," the woman said. "Let's get you out of here. You must be hungry after your long journey!"

Gallant didn't understand her words, but he appreciated her kindness and he allowed her to lead him down the ramp and onto the gravel driveway that led to the barn. When he saw the two men who had treated him so roughly he snorted and pinned his ears back in their direction.

"He was a real monster to load, Miss Jenny," the one man said. "You need to keep an eye on him!"

Gallant flinched at the memory of the sting of the whip on his legs and wondered if there were others like them here.

As Jenny led him away from the men, Gallant looked around at his new surroundings. There was a very long building, much larger than the barn back home, with several exterior runs, all with doors that entered stalls along the whole length of the building. The roof was pitched and at the end was a large pair of doors that slid open. Once inside, Gallant could see a huge open space in the middle of the barn surrounded by fencing. The space was separated from the pens by a wide breezeway. Horses of various sizes and colors poked their heads curiously over the pen gates, staring at the latest newcomer.

"Let's get you settled into a nice warm stall of your own so you can eat and drink," Jenny said.

She led Gallant into an empty stall with fresh shavings on the floor and a tub full of cool water in one corner. There was a flake of sweet-smelling hay inside a manger and Gallant could not wait to dig into it. He was so hungry! He hadn't eaten since before the accident yesterday afternoon. Once inside the stall, the woman gently removed the red halter from his head and hung it over a hook outside the stall door. "OK, Gallant," she said, "this is your new home for a while. You and I will be working together a lot from now on, so relax for a couple of days and then our work will begin."

Jenny stepped outside the stall and disappeared back down the aisle way, leaving Gallant to settle into the new space. At first, he was so hungry and thirsty that he didn't even have time to think about where he was, or what he was doing there. He drank deeply from the water tub and then dove his head into the fresh hay. He didn't stop eating until nearly all the hay was gone and his belly finally felt satisfied. Only then did he begin to look around and really notice his surroundings.

Next to him on one side was a bay stallion with a wide blaze of white running from his forehead to his muzzle. His coloring was similar to Gallant's, but his size and power made Gallant seem small in comparison. Instead of falling to one side, his mane was short and stuck up in a mohawk along his neckline. His eyes were hard and unfriendly. Gallant tentatively moved toward him and the bay arched his neck and touched Gallant's nose with his own. He sniffed Gallant for a few moments before squealing and stomping his right foot onto the floor of his stall. Gallant stepped back, his eyes opening wider as he looked at the bay in confusion. Behind him he heard a soft nicker of laughter and turned to see a chestnut filly watching him.

"Don't mind him! That's Flash. He's sort of the boss around here, but he's not mean or anything. He just wants to let you know who's in charge!" the pretty little filly said. "I'm Marinera, by the way," she continued. "Welcome to Greenhill Training Stables. Where are you from?"

Gallant moved toward Marinera since she was far more friendly and less intimidating than Flash, who had returned to eating his hay, ignoring the newcomer.

"I'm Gallant," he told her. "I'm from the Valley of Heart's Delight. I have no idea where I am or why I'm here. I think that maybe I did a terrible thing to my human friend yesterday and I might have been brought here as punishment, or maybe she's here as well and will be coming to find me soon." Gallant scraped the floor with his hoof and dropped his head lower. "I've never been away from my home before," he said sadly. "I really wish I just knew where Gracie was."

Marinera nodded in understanding. "I know how you feel, Gallant. I was brought here three months ago and haven't seen my mother, or any of my friends from back home this whole time. They do take good care of you here, though, and give you plenty of fresh hay and water, and if you do well in your lessons you sometimes get a special treat in a bucket! It's not all bad."

Gallant wasn't sure if Marinera was telling the truth or if she was just trying to make him feel better, but he appreciated her friendship. "What do you mean by lessons?" he asked.

"Oh," Marinera replied. "It's a bit strange at first because they make you run around in circles at the end of a long rope, and you have to go as fast or as slow as they tell you with the whip."

Gallant shuddered as he thought about the whip the men had used to scare him into the trailer. He didn't like the sound of being chased around by that again.

"Then they put these funny metal things in your mouth, and they put a heavy thing on your back and strap it around your belly," Marinera continued. "If you do good with that, they sit on you!"

The memory of Gracie leading him over to the mounting block, and the feeling of her weight on his back suddenly made things clear to him. Gracie had been trying to sit on his back so she could ride him, and instead of letting her he had run away, and Gracie had been injured. Oh, if only he had understood what she had been trying to do he would have let her sit on him for as long as she wanted. Gallant realized that Gracie had been trying to find a way to spend more time with him. That it could have been *him* that she would take out in the middle of the night to ride in the moonlight instead of Andy. How stupid he had been! He wished he could go back to yesterday and do everything all over again. He would have stood there like a good horse and let Gracie do whatever she wanted. He would have carried her up and down the orchard all day and all night if she had wanted him to. Now it was too late.

Gallant stood in his stall with his head hanging low, no longer interested in talking to the pretty little filly who eventually went back to eating her own hay. She sensed that the newcomer had a lot of things on his mind and needed to be left alone for a while. Soon all the lights in the barn went out, and the horses stopped munching on their last few bites of hay and got ready to settle down for the night. Some circled and pawed at the ground until they found a place to lay down. Others just stood and rested.

The last thing Gallant saw before falling into an exhausted sleep was the bright circle of a full moon shining through the skylight on the roof of the barn. *Maybe that is the same moon that Gracie can see*, he thought. He closed his eyes and tried to imagine he was back at home, where he could see his mother in the paddock next to him, and the lights of the ranch house reassuring him that Gracie and her family were close by. He could almost see the shadows of the pear trees in the orchard, and the smell of the mustard grass that swayed in the breeze. Gallant decided that every night he would look up at the moon and remember all the times he and Gracie had spent together. The moon would connect them through this time apart, and maybe one day it would even guide them back to each other. With that last thought, Gallant fell into a restless sleep.

Chapter Six

A PART OF HER

When Gracie awoke, she was lying in a hospital bed in San Jose, the closest hospital to the Valley of Heart's Delight. Her parents were sitting on either side of her bed, both looking at her anxiously. Her mother held her hand and asked her if she remembered anything about what had happened. Gracie shook her head slowly. Her head hurt, and her chin was covered in a bulky dressing with tape over it. She could feel that her right side was bruised, and her wrist hurt, but the worst pain was coming from her ankle. When she tried to wiggle her toes, a sharp pain shot up her leg, and she winced and sucked in her breath at the shock of it. The lower part of her leg was in a hard cast.

"What happened?" she asked, looking from one parent to the next.

"You had some hair-brained idea to try and ride that young gelding you've been hanging around with," her father said gruffly. Her mother shot him a look that told him to calm down, that this was not the time to be getting angry with his daughter. His gaze softened and he reached down and took Gracie's other hand, careful not to move her sprained wrist.

"You scared us, Gracie," he said more gently. "We thought we had lost you. We heard you scream and came running out the house and there you were, just lying on the ground with blood pouring from your chin and your legs all tangled up. That damn horse was almost standing on top of you. Your mother could hardly get him to move away so we could carry you to the house while we waited for the ambulance."

Gracie's eyes started to tear up as she began remembering. "It was my fault, Daddy!" she said urgently. "I was trying to get Gallant ready to ride at Buckingham palace with the Queen! We needed to practice! He just didn't understand what I was trying to do. I promise I'll be more careful next time."

Roy blamed himself that his daughter was still carrying around fanciful notions in her head about taking her horse to England to ride with the Queen. It was time that Gracie grew up and focused on the realities of life, living in the real world instead of make-believe. But now was not the time to tell Gracie that the horse had been removed from the property. He and Harriet had agreed to have Gallant taken to their trainer in the foothills near Auburn so he could begin the training that should have started years ago. Both her parents knew it was unlikely that Gallant would be suitable for Gracie to ride for several years. Gracie would be far better off with a seasoned trail horse that had no aspirations of racing around in a manner that could get a child hurt.

Tears began running down Gracie's cheeks, wetting the pillow on either side of her bruised face. "Daddy, honestly, it was my fault! Please don't be mad at Gallant! He must have been so scared as well. I should have explained things better to him and taken it slower. Please, Daddy."

Roy loved his daughter, and although not usually a man to show public displays of affection, he sat at the edge of her bed and tried to soothe her, running his hand across her forehead and then wiping the tears from her face.

"There, there," he said. "Let's not worry about it now. We've all had a long day. The doctor says that if you have a good night's sleep tonight, and everything looks good in the morning, you can be released to go home. We can talk more about this once we get you settled back into your own room at the ranch."

Gracie took a few staggered breaths, trying to calm her tears, and gave her parents a tentative smile. "Yes, Daddy," she nodded. "I will do everything the doctors tell me to so that I am able to go home tomorrow. I can't bear to be so far away from Gallant, and Fling, and our beautiful Valley of Heart's Delight any longer. I am so sorry that I scared you both."

Harriet gave her youngest daughter a hug. "Daddy and I have to get home to your sister and brother now, but the nice nurses here will take very good care of you, and we will be back in the morning to help you get ready to leave. I'm sorry this happened on your birthday, Gracie. We'll save your cake to have tomorrow when you come home, okay?"

Her parents stood and after one last reassuring smile at their daughter they left. A nurse came in to take Gracie's temperature and check her bandages, then offered her a rather inedible tray of hospital food. Gracie's chin hurt so much that she couldn't open her mouth very far, so she ended up just eating a small bowl of Jell-O and nibbling on half a peanut butter sandwich. Her stomach felt queasy, either from the accident or from worrying about Gallant, she wasn't sure which.

When the nurse came to turn off the lights later that evening, she handed Gracie a Hershey bar and said with a wink, "A little bird told me these are your favorites and that it is your birthday today! Bedtime isn't exactly the best time to eat chocolate, but with the day you've had, I think we can make an exception!"

Gracie fell asleep planning everything she would say to Gallant the next day when she saw him again. She would find a way to get over to the barn and into his stall, broken ankle or not, and she would wrap her arms around his neck and tell him how sorry she was, that she would never push him that hard again to do something new. She would give him some time to get over the incident while her leg healed, and then she would ask her father if she could do some extra work in the pear orchard that summer to earn money for proper riding lessons so she would know how to better help Gallant when she was able to try riding him again.

Feeling that at least she now had a plan, Gracie fell asleep. In her dream she was in Gallant's stall, but he was looking at her with fear in his eyes and would not come over to her. When she reached toward him, he started shaking all over, and Gracie could only back away and curl up in the corner of his stall, hoping that eventually he would be comfortable enough to seek her out. She woke early in the morning, crying out for him. He was her best friend and she felt that what had happened might somehow change their relationship. What if Gallant didn't trust her anymore? She had promised him the day he was born that she would always take care of him, and now she felt that she had broken that promise. Gallant was the one who always listened to her when she was mad, or scared, or just needed to talk. Who would listen to her, if not him? Gracie realized in that moment how much a part of her Gallant had become. Not just a part of her life, but a part of *her*. They depended on each other for so much more than friendship. Every day their lives weaved seamlessly together, like the braids she wove into his mane. Without Gallant's love, Gracie wasn't sure who she was anymore.

Before long, the light began pouring through the curtains of the hospital window. Gracie was tired but determined to go home and start making right the wrongs from the previous day. Everything *had* to be alright. She and Gallant were a team and they needed each other.

Gracie lay there waiting for the nurse to help her get dressed so she could be ready to leave when her parents arrived. It was awkward trying to move as her whole right side was bruised and sore, and the cast on her ankle made it difficult to stand. The nurse reassured her that the pain would ease up over the next few days, and that she would learn how to use crutches so she could get around without putting too much weight on her bad ankle. The cast would come off in a matter of weeks, depending how the healing progressed.

By the time her parents arrived, Gracie was ready to go. The doctor came and gave her one last examination.

"Children tend to heal very quickly," he reassured them. "But do encourage her to keep that leg elevated for several hours a day the first two weeks." Then he looked at Gracie, "After that, young lady, you may do whatever is comfortable for you. You'll know when you have pushed yourself too far."

"How soon can I ride my horse?" Gracie asked the doctor. She didn't notice her parents' quick intake of breath at the question. The doctor sat down on the bed next to Gracie and answered her very seriously.

"Gracie, you have suffered quite a bad fracture of your ankle. It could take months before you can even walk without a limp and your body needs time to recover from the trauma of your fall. You are a very lucky little girl as it could have been worse if your head had taken a harder hit. You need to listen to me when I tell you there will be no riding horses for at least the next four months.

Maybe even six, depending on how your body heals. Do you understand what I am saying?"

Gracie nodded solemnly. Somehow, she would find a way to spend time with Gallant. She could still sit with him in his stall, groom him, and talk to him about her day, just like she always had. When she started to get better and didn't need the crutches anymore, she would be able to lead him around the stable area, and even to the orchard.

During the car ride, her bad ankle stretched out between the front seats, she focused on how much closer to home she was getting, and how happy she would be once she got there. Her father had picked her up in the nice Sunday car rather than the work truck so she could stretch out and be more comfortable, and it was quite a treat to be the only one in the back seat, rather than crammed between her brother and sister. As the car turned down the long driveway Gracie gazed at her beloved pear trees. She tried not to be too sad that she wouldn't be able to enjoy them from the back of her pony, but she was grateful to be back here, where she belonged.

The car continued down the driveway and past the stables. Gracie strained to see out the window, hoping to catch a glimpse of Gallant in his paddock, but she could only see Magri and her foal grazing. He must be in the stable, she thought. He wouldn't think it was me coming home in this car. He's only used to the sound of the work truck, and the school bus. But she craned her neck, nonetheless, hoping that he might emerge after all.

Her focus was distracted by the sight of her brother and sister coming out of the house and running to the car. Fling was close on their heels, barking excitedly. Nancy pulled the door open and was about to envelop Gracie in a big hug when her mother cautioned, "Wait, Nancy! I know you've been worried about Gracie, but you will have to be very careful around her for a while or you could hurt her."

Nancy took a closer look at Gracie and saw the dressing on her chin, the bruising running down her arm and wrist and the cast on her ankle. She pulled back, apologizing to her sister, "You poor thing!" she stated. "Don't you worry. We are all going to take excellent care of you and help you get better! Bill even picked some pretty flowers for your room so you can close your eyes and imagine you are laying in a garden of wildflowers up in the hills!"

Gracie smiled. Apparently, all it took was an accident to finally get her siblings' attention. Her father came around to the back of the car and instructed Nancy and Bill to grab anything of Gracie's and carry it up to her room. Then he put his strong arms under Gracie's legs and around her back, lifting her easily out of the car. "All those years of hauling boxes of pears in from the orchard have paid off!" he said, smiling.

Gracie rested her head against his chest and inhaled his scent. It was a mixture of soap and shaving cream, always with the underlying subtle smell of the soil. It made her feel safe. She knew she would never forget the scent for as long as she lived. Roy wasn't always the most demonstrative man, but Gracie knew without a doubt that his first priority in life was his family. She hugged herself closer to him and whispered, "Thank you for taking such good care of me, Daddy." His arms tightened around her.

Within minutes Gracie was tucked into her own bed and her mother had brought her a plate of her favorite chicken soup made with sweet baby carrots from her garden. The family sat around her while she ate. Once she was finished, Bill and Nancy ran downstairs and came back with the birthday cake from yesterday. They all sang "Happy Birthday" to her and laughed when she couldn't purse her lips to blow out the candle because of the dressing still on her chin. With her siblings' help, they blew out the candles and everyone had a slice of cake.

"Okay, you two, your mother and I need to have a chat with Gracie so take the dirty plates downstairs and you can come and say goodnight a little bit later," Roy said, looking at Nancy and Bill.

Once they left the room, Harriet glanced sideways at her husband. "Let's just let Gracie settle in today, Roy. We can talk with her in the morning."

Roy looked at Harriet and shook his head. "Gracie needs to know where we stand on this, Harriet, so the sooner we get this conversation over with, the better."

Harriet knew that as much as they both loved Gracie the conversation they were about to have with her was going to be painful. Roy was insistent. The sooner she knew of their decision, the sooner she could begin to wrap her head around it.

"Gracie," her mother said softly, "we blame ourselves for what happened the other day. It was not your fault, and it was not Gallant's fault. We left you two virtually unsupervised all these years because we could see what a special bond you had with each other. We wanted you to enjoy time with your horse, but we should have put a stop to it sooner, when Gallant became almost full-grown. Young horses are strong and can be unpredictable. We know he would never have hurt you intentionally, but we also knew there was a risk that you *might* get hurt eventually."

Gracie looked at her mother with questioning eyes. What was her mother saying? That Gracie could only visit with Gallant if she were supervised? She supposed she could deal with that if she had to, although she worried that her mother would be too busy to take her out to the stable very often. Then her father spoke.

"Gracie, the fact is that you will not be able to ride for many months, and we don't want you to be tempted to try as you start feeling better. We have found a family a few miles away that will take Andy. They have a little boy that wants a pony, and they will give him a good home."

Gracie's eyes teared up at the thought of her little black and white pony belonging to someone other than her, but that was nothing compared to the shock of what her father said next.

"And Gracie, Gallant is already gone."

Chapter Seven

WE WON'T RISK YOU BEING HURT AGAIN

Gracie's mind was numb. She could not fathom that Gallant was not just across the way, at the barn, like he had been for the past five years of her life. She would not be able to see him cantering toward her in the paddock or smell his sweet horse smell as she wrapped her arms around his neck and told him all her secrets. How could he be gone? She hadn't even had the chance to say goodbye to him. And what was Gallant thinking? That he had been sent away as a punishment even though he had done nothing wrong? It had all been *her* fault! *She* was the one who had asked too much of him. She hadn't explained to him what she was planning to do. He had just been surprised, that's all. Gallant would never want to hurt her. He must be so sad and lost, wondering where she was. Gracie's parents, who she knew loved her beyond measure, had also broken her heart. She could barely speak.

"Where is he?" she managed to say in a strangled voice, her throat dry and tight with grief.

Harriet reached for her daughter, concerned that she was suddenly so pale and so shaken. "He's only up in the foothills at the training stables, Gracie. He's not gone for good, just for a few months. Jenny, the trainer, will let us know how he does, and if it seems like he has a good mind and will be a safe horse for our family he can come back home. By then your ankle should have healed." Harriet glanced over at her husband. "But Gracie, if Jenny doesn't feel that he is safe for either you or I to ride he will have to be sold. We won't risk you being hurt again."

Gracie looked from one parent to the other, her eyes still full of tears. This was not as bad as she had first thought, though. Her mother had said he would be back once he had learned his lessons. Gallant was smart and would work hard, she just knew it! He would probably learn faster than any other horse at the training stables and be back even sooner than they expected, but oh, how she would miss him in the meantime. Gracie could not even imagine being without him for even one day.

Gracie was a sensible child and she understood that her parents had her, and Gallant's, best interests at heart. She had often heard her mother say that the biggest disservice you could do to a horse was not to train it and give it a job. Untrained horses tended to pass through the hands of many owners until hopefully they found one with enough time and experience to teach them properly. If they never got that opportunity their fate could be disastrous. Gracie knew that Gallant needed training, and that he would be a better horse for it. After taking a deep breath to calm herself she looked up at her parents.

"I understand. I really do. I will miss Gallant, but I will focus on getting my leg better and doing well in school. And when I can, Daddy, I would like to do some extra work in the orchards this season so that I can earn some money and help pay toward Gallant's training. I will pay you back every penny, I promise."

Roy smiled at his daughter.

"I'm proud of you, Gracie," her father said. "Let's just take one day at a time and focus on your recovery. Don't forget, Fling has missed you a lot while you were at the hospital and he could do with some extra attention over the next few weeks!"

Gracie smiled at Fling who had made himself comfortable next to her bed, his head resting next to Gracie's hand on top of the covers. She reached over to pet him.

"Yes, Fling and I will have some special time together," she agreed.

The dog seemed to understand what she was saying and wagged his tail, hitting the side of the bed rhythmically with each movement. He pressed his head further under Gracie's hand and nuzzled closer to her, happy to be getting some attention. Gracie laughed, and her parents breathed a sigh of relief that the conversation they had been dreading had gone reasonably well.

Gracie made the most of having to stay in bed the first few days she was back home by having her siblings, who were still sympathetic to her plight, willing to do whatever she asked. Any time she needed something she rang the little bell next to her bedside and one of them would come running. But after the first few days the novelty of having a sister who needed a lot of help wore off, and Gracie found herself more and more alone with her thoughts, and with Fling, her ever faithful companion. After the first few days, Gracie's parents felt that she'd had enough bedrest and could now be brought downstairs. To make things easier, her father and brother carried her bed down and set it up in the living room, so that Gracie did not have to go up and down the stairs with her crutches the first few weeks.

The day soon came when Gracie had mastered the crutches enough to get outside into the fresh air. She was excited to be going out where she could explore parts of her beautiful ranch again, but she knew that she would have to see Gallant's empty stall and paddock, and that was going to make his absence seem all the more real.

Gracie hobbled toward the barn, already experiencing a sinking feeling in the pit of her stomach. She saw Gallant's paddock, but no Gallant running over to greet her. Fling was by her side as always, ever vigilant, and careful not to get in her way and risk tripping her. He had taken on the task of being her constant companion and dog-nurse during her healing process, and without his comforting presence next to her, Gracie knew she would have struggled far more with her confinement.

Gracie made her way across to the paddock and stood there for a moment, trying to imagine Gallant was there, running around kicking up his heels and making her laugh. She remembered how he would chase the leaves floating down from the treetops, trying to nudge them with his nose as they fell, and then stomping them into the ground dramatically. Gracie wondered if he would be different when he came back from the trainers. Maybe he would be all grown up while she was still a child.

She went into the barn and to Magri's stall. Magri immediately came up to her, nickering a question, looking for, and offering reassurance.

"It's okay, Magri. Gallant will be back in a few months. He's learning how to be ridden and how to be a grown-up horse, and then we will all be able to go on rides together, you and Mother, me and Gallant. It will be wonderful!"

Magri leaned into Gracie's touch, feeling the connection to her son through this girl that he loved. Her trust and need broke down Gracie's walls and the tears began to pour down her cheeks.

"I miss him, Magri. I miss him so much! I am trying to be brave, but I feel this big, empty hole inside and I don't know how to fill it! I talk to Fling every night, and I love him, I really do, but nothing is the same as being with Gallant. How will I ever get through these next months without him?"

Magri stood there, allowing the girl to break, feeling the moment her tears started to ebb and her breathing settled. Gracie wiped her tear-stained face on Magri's mane. She felt better now that she had been able to get how she felt off her chest. She offered the mare a slight smile. "Thank you for listening to me, Magri, and being here for me. I can see where Gallant got his kind nature. Maybe you and I can become even better friends now. I know that you miss him too."

Gracie turned, ready to go back inside and rest after what seemed like a long journey to the barn. When she got back to the house, she searched out her mother. "Can we call Jenny and see how Gallant is doing with his training so far?" she asked.

Harriet looked away from her daughter briefly. She had been in touch with Jenny already and knew that Gallant had arrived safely at Greenhill Training Stables, but he had not been eating well and appeared to be very homesick. Jenny had reassured Harriet that some horses took longer than others to adjust to new surroundings and she would give him an extra couple of days to settle in before starting to work with him. Harriet did not want Gracie to be present at a phone call until she knew there was some good news to report. "I've already spoken to Jenny, and she says that Gallant arrived safely, and she will start working with him soon. She asked that we give her a month or so before calling for updates on his progress so that she has had a chance to work with him first, so we'll check in with her then, okay? It's a lovely facility and I am sure he's making new friends already!"

Gracie looked disappointed but nodded in agreement. "Gallant is so smart, and he'll want to do well so he can come home sooner. I just know it!" she responded.

Over the next few days Gracie went outside more and more often. She was really starting to get the hang of the crutches and Fling would run a few steps ahead of her, turning around to bark his encouragement, making Gracie laugh. She was determined to get her strength back so she would be ready to ride Gallant when he finally came home. So long as she focused on that, the emptiness inside her did not consume her thoughts, and if it did, she would repeat to herself, *focus on Gallant*, and the darkness would stay in the distance.

Chapter Eight

THE FAILURE OF HIS FIRST LESSON

Gallant had been at the training facility for two weeks now. He and Marinera had become friends, but Flash was another story. Usually Flash just ignored him, but on the rare occasion that he spoke, it was always to put Gallant down in some way. Marinera had been right, the horses there were well taken care of. They received plenty of fresh, sweet hay and clean water every day. They were lacking for nothing physically, with large runs that allowed them to be outside in the fresh air whenever they felt like it, and stalls for warmth and shelter at night.

The two men, Larry and Ted, who had brought Gallant to the facility were responsible for cleaning the stalls every day. Gallant always moved as far away from them as possible when they entered his stall. He didn't trust either of them, especially with a pitchfork in their hands. So far, they hadn't tried to touch him again, but he didn't like the feeling he got when they were close by.

The hairs on his coat stood up and his skin pricked as if something bad was about to happen.

Gallant found that each day he grew more and more homesick for Gracie, his mother, and the Valley of Heart's Delight. His homesickness made him less interested in his food, and when he didn't eat his energy dwindled and he spent most of his time just standing around. Sometimes he would go outside, but instead of running and kicking up his heels like he did at home, he would meander slowly around his pen and then stand against the fence line that bordered Marinera's and find what comfort he could from being next to her.

Marinera was concerned about her new stable mate and couldn't understand why he wasn't enjoying himself more. "Gallant," she said softly one evening, "You won't be here forever, you know. Horses are sent here for training and eventually they all go home. Unless they are here to be sold. Which I am sure is not the case for you," she added quickly when Gallant looked up in alarm. "Why don't you try and enjoy your time here? Jenny is very nice. Even Flash isn't so bad once you get to know him!"

Gallant glanced over at Flash who looked back at him, flattening his ears against his head as he did so. "Oh yes," said Gallant, "I can tell Flash and I are going to be best buddies!"

Marinera snorted in amusement. "Well, you do almost look like you could be brothers. You're the same color, and you both have white markings on your head and legs. Are you sure your parents didn't know each other?"

"Don't even say that Marinera!" Gallant responded, but Marinera had done what she intended and had shocked Gallant out of his lethargy.

For several hours during the day there was activity in the arena and sometimes Gallant's inquisitiveness would get the better of him. He would watch as Jenny worked with several of the horses she had in training. He was especially interested if she was working with Marinera or Flash. Marinera had advanced enough in her training that she was being ridden every day now. First Albert, the groom, would come and get her from her stall. She would be tied up in the grooming area and brushed. Her feet would be picked up and Albert would scrape any mud or dirt off the bottom of her hooves, making sure there were no stones lodged in there that could make her uncomfortable as she moved. Then a pad would be thrown across her back and a saddle put on top of that. A girth was strung underneath her belly and attached to each side of the saddle to hold it in place. Her halter would be removed, and she would be asked to accept the bit—a steel bar about four or five inches wide that was attached to a bridle. Once Marinera accepted the bit, the bridle was looped over her ears, and then reins were attached to either side of the bit. Gallant could see that the reins had something to do with how the rider communicated instructions to the horse, and

Marinera had told him that while the bit felt funny at first she had soon become used to it.

Watching the two of them in the arena, Gallant could see that Jenny was using both her legs and her hands to communicate to Marinera, even shifting her position on the horse slightly every now and again to further help Marinera learn what was being asked of her. When it was Flash's turn to be ridden, Gallant could see that the more experienced horse moved with far more confidence, circling, turning, stepping away at a diagonal, coming to a complete halt with barely any movement from his rider that Gallant could see. It was like a dance between them, invisible strings controlling Flash's movements as he flowed and shifted beneath his rider. When Flash returned to his stall, he would look at Gallant as if to say, "Watch and weep. You will never be as good as me!"

Gallant was curious what it would feel like to be ridden, but he only wanted to be ridden by Gracie. He had twisted the circumstances of the accident around so much in his mind that he felt the only way he could make it up to Gracie was by making sure she was the only one to ever ride him.

When Jenny decided that Gallant had done enough moping around, he was presented to her in the arena by the groom, having been brushed and having had his feet cleaned and checked. Jenny had a very long, flat rope looped around her arm. He recognized it from seeing the other horses being moved in circles while Jenny stood in the middle.

"Thank you, Albert," she nodded as he handed the lead rope to her. She dropped the flat rope onto the ground and stepped closer to Gallant.

Gallant looked around and could see many of the horses looking over the doors of their stalls at him, wondering how he would do at his first lesson in the arena. Marinera whinnied her encouragement to him while Flash stood there staring, no expression in his eye.

Jenny began to touch Gallant all over with her hands, talking to him in low gentle tones as she ran her hands down his neck, his front legs, and eventually under his belly. Gallant was used to Gracie doing all of that, so it didn't bother him. He stood quietly, waiting to see what Jenny would do next. Jenny looked toward Albert, giving him a subtle nod, and he approached with a whip that looked like the one the men had used to chase Gallant into the trailer the night they had taken him away from his home. Gallant moved his feet nervously, watching the whip out of the corner of his eye. All he could remember was how scared he had been when the men had waved it behind him, and the sharp sting of it on his legs. He had felt trapped and threatened, a feeling he had never experienced before, and the memory was still fresh in his mind.

Gallant saw the whip moving closer toward him. He waited for the sting he had felt last time and his body shook in anticipation of the pain he would surely feel.

He could hear Jenny's calm voice reassuring him, but the moment she gently touched the whip against his neck to show him that it wouldn't hurt, Gallant reacted. His feet exploded off the ground and he reared up, pulling the lead rope out of Jenny's hand. His terrified mind screamed "danger!" and he took off at a run, trying to get as far away from the whip as he could. He was trapped in the arena, so he ran from one end to the other, nostrils flaring, breath coming out in heaving snorts, tail lifted in the air behind him as he flew up and down in the confined space.

Gallant could see Jenny standing in the middle of the arena watching him. She dropped the whip at her feet and moved away from it, realizing that for some reason it had triggered a huge amount of fear in the young horse. Gallant finally tired of running and came to a halt at one end of the arena, his body shaking, breaking out with a sweat that left trails of white foam down his neck and beneath his tail. As his breathing slowed, he looked around and saw, to his horror, that the horses still had their heads hanging over their stall doors watching him.

"That was quite the show you put on there," one horse whinnied to him.

"Imagine what he'll do when she tries to put a saddle on him!" another said.

Gallant wanted to tell them his fear was valid. He had been hurt before, but he realized they probably didn't care. They just saw him as a big baby who knew nothing and feared everything. He turned to Jenny as she reached her hand toward him and spoke in a soothing voice.

"Easy now, there's nothing to be scared of here."

Gallant needed a friend. He needed to feel safe and loved, and he didn't like feeling alone. He remembered how gentle Jenny had been with him the night he had arrived, and how soft her hands had felt as she ran them over his body earlier. His head lowered and he took a tentative step toward her.

"That's it, Gallant, come here to me," Jenny said, and waited, knowing that when he was ready, he would come to her.

Gallant took a step closer, reaching out to her with his muzzle, letting his body follow until he was close enough for Jenny to reach the lead rope. She stood there for a while with him, allowing him to calm down and process what had happened, then she quietly ran her hands over his body once again, wanting him to leave the lesson with a feeling of safety and trust. Gallant knew that Jenny understood that he had this terrible fear. She didn't know why, but she had recognized it and understood how hard it had been for him. Gallant wasn't sure why he had reacted so dramatically. He sensed that Jenny would never hurt him, it was just that his brain seemed to shut down in that moment and all he could remember when he saw the whip was the pain—the pain of that day he was taken away from his home. Gallant walked back to the grooming area with Jenny, and she gently brushed the dried sweat out of his coat. Then she took him back to his stall and removed his halter.

"We'll try again tomorrow Gallant," she said, patting his neck, and walked away.

Gallant could not look the others in the eye. He was so embarrassed at how he had reacted, showing such fear in front of the horses watching from their stalls. Marinera tried to comfort him, but he turned away, unable to face her and feeling deeply ashamed. Even Flash did not make fun of him, seeing how truly miserable he was standing alone in the corner of his stall.

The failure of his first lesson only added to his feeling of homesickness. He wondered if he would ever feel happy again. Maybe Gracie hadn't loved him as much as he'd thought. It was obvious now that she would not be coming to get him, or even to visit. Or maybe he had hurt her so badly that she *couldn't* come to see him. She was probably glad that such a dangerous horse was off her property and maybe she had even found another horse to talk to and spend time with by now. Gallant wondered where his life could possibly go from here.

Chapter Nine

EAT UP, WEAKLING

G allant woke the next day with a new determination to do better in his lessons, and to build on the friendships he was starting to make with his barn mates. He walked over to Marinera who was eating her breakfast and put his head over the divider between their stalls.

"I'm so sorry for how I acted yesterday, Marinera. I didn't mean to ignore you when you spoke to me, I was just so embarrassed about what happened," he told her.

Marinera moved towards him and touched his muzzle with her own. "It's perfectly okay, Gallant," she replied. "It was your first lesson. We all get better as time goes on. I wanted you to know that you are safe with Jenny. She won't hurt you. She's just training you so that you will be a better horse for your owner," she explained.

"I know," Gallant said, grateful that he had a friend to talk to. "I will do better next time, I promise."

Marinera nodded. "I have never seen a horse run so fast though! I bet you could win some races with speed like that!"

Gallant relaxed, even chuckling slightly at the memory of himself running frantically up and down the arena. When his legs started moving, they could certainly produce amazing bursts of speed. Gracie had loved seeing him running and bucking, and the young horse would gladly show off for her, jumping over fallen tree limbs and weaving in and out of the gopher holes. His young body had learned how to navigate all the natural obstacles in his paddock, while his lungs had expanded and strengthened during the times he had followed Gracie on the trails through the hills. He could run for what seemed like forever without getting tired at all.

Gallant noticed that Flash was not in his pen, nor was he in the arena having a lesson. He asked Marinera if she knew where he was.

"Oh, yes!" she said. "He is training out on the trails today. He gets to be ridden over the hills and valleys around the ranch now. He says he is going to be a famous endurance horse."

"Wow!" Gallant exclaimed. "My mother, Magri, was ridden all over the hills around our ranch at home. Does that make her an endurance horse as well?" he asked Marinera.

"I don't know," she replied, looking at Gallant quizzically, "She might have been. Did she go to races and stuff? Endurance horses must go very long distances and compete against other horses to see who wins. Sometimes they get prizes like new blankets to wear, or a new feed bucket. I'm not sure I would want to run that far just to get a new feed bucket, but I hear some horses really love it!"

Gallant thought about what Marinera had said. He knew he had been sent here to learn how to be ridden, and it made sense that Jenny would also be looking to see what kind of job he could do in the future. Some of her horses were learning how to go over jumps while others were being taught how to be good trail-riding horses, and now Flash was apparently being conditioned for endurance.

When Flash returned to his stall several hours later Gallant approached him, curious to learn more about what being an endurance horse was all about. Flash looked a little tired but very happy, which was an unusual look for him.

Gallant sidled up to their shared fence line and watched Flash voraciously eating his bucket of special grain and supplements. Sweet alfalfa hay filled his manger, a reward for his hard work, and a necessity to replenish his body from the miles he had put in on the trails that day. Flash's coat was clean and shiny from being bathed, and stretched tightly over the shape of his musculature, built up from many hours of being under saddle.

Gallant nickered softly to alert Flash that he was standing by, hoping to talk to him. Flash barely glanced his way.

"So, Flash," Gallant started to say with great hesitation, not wanting to make the other horse angry. "I was wondering if you could tell me more about what it takes to be an endurance horse. Marinera told me that is what you're training for."

Flash turned his head and looked at Gallant. This was a subject he liked, and since he had licked the bottom of his bucket clean, he approached Gallant saying,

"Sure, I can tell you a few things. At my barn back home there are several of us endurance horses. We are the best athletes, we can run the farthest, the hardest, and for the longest. My sire is one of the top endurance horses in the country and has won some of the most difficult races the humans have challenged us with. It takes training, stamina, and a will to conquer any mountain that is put in front of you. It can take years before a horse has a chance of becoming the best. I plan on being as good as, if not better than my sire, and then I will take his place as the Lead stallion at our barn, and I will get to breed to all of the best mares to produce future champions."

Gallant looked at Flash with even more awe than usual. "Who will ride you in these races, Flash?" he asked.

"I don't care!" Flash snorted. "As long as they can stay on and not hold me back. That's all I care about."

Gallant thought about what Flash had said. It seemed to him that if you were going to be ridden all those miles it would be much better to be ridden by someone who cared about you. Surely being with someone you had a special bond with would make all those hours of training and racing even more fun. Gallant wondered whether he could be an endurance horse. He thought of Gracie and how much she liked to ride her pony up and down between the pear trees in the orchard, and how he would run with them into the hills behind their home. He was pretty sure that Gracie would love riding in endurance races, and it would mean they could spend even more time together. Think of all the adventure's they could have!

"Flash, do you think I could be an endurance horse?" he asked eagerly.

Flash looked him up and down and started to laugh.

"You?" he sneered. "You haven't even been ridden yet and your legs are not the right shape to carry you for long miles. You would get hurt too easily."

Gallant looked down at his legs. He had never had a problem with them. "What do you mean?" he asked, confused by Flash's words.

Flash sighed. He was losing patience with this conversation since it was no longer about him.

"Your pasterns are too long . . . that would be your ankles," he explained. "Your back legs are too straight. There's not enough angle to them. You won't have the power to climb long hills. Endurance horses need to be able to carry their riders over miles of open space, across all kinds of terrain. Just because you can run fast in a paddock, or up and down an arena doesn't mean that you can carry the weight of a person for fifty miles or more on a cross-country trail. People put a lot of time into our training, so they don't want to start out with a horse that is built all wrong in the first place. I'm sure there's something else they can use you for, Gallant. Maybe you can give pony rides at children's parties."

After delivering that blow, Flash moved away to start tucking into his alfalfa. Gallant stood there quietly for a moment absorbing everything Flash had said. Despite Flash being grumpy and unneighborly Gallant had looked up to him after seeing how beautifully he moved under saddle in the arena. Flash was large and powerful. He seemed like he wouldn't be scared of anything, and yet Gallant had spent half an hour yesterday running away from a whip! Flash probably ate whips for breakfast. Knowing that Flash had been out there for hours training in the mountains had boosted Gallant's admiration for the large bay stallion even more. Flash seemed to understand the world and his place in it so much better he did. What Flash had said must be true. There was no reason for Gallant to doubt him.

Gallant moved back to the center of his stall and hung his head, feeling completely defeated. For just a moment he had dared to dream. He could think of nothing better than riding across mountains and through rivers with Gracie on his back as they raced toward a finish line miles away. For a moment, his thoughts of being an endurance horse had seemed so real that he imagined he may have found his place in the world. A place where Gracie could be right there with him. Now his hopes were dashed.

Later that afternoon Ted and Larry came in to clean the stalls. Ted began with Marinera's stall while Larry entered Gallant's. Gallant had been miserable all day after his conversation with Flash. He kept hearing Flash's words in his head. Gallant snorted when he realized that Larry was getting closer to him with the pitchfork. Larry smelled funny, and he seemed a little wobbly on his feet.

"The big baby is looking sadder than usual today, Ted. Maybe he needs a pacifier, or someone to change his big baby diaper," Larry said, laughing.

"Maybe he's sad because he can't come in here with his girlfriend!" Ted yelled back.

"Bring her over here so he can take a good look at her," Larry drawled. Ted began to manhandle Marinera, grabbing her by her mane and trying to drag her closer to where Gallant was standing in his stall. She whinnied frantically, uncomfortable with the way the man was touching her and not understanding their words. When she didn't move, Ted began smacking her on her rump with the pitchfork. Marinera tried to get away from him, running around her stall in a panic while Ted kept lunging at her, laughing at her fear.

Gallant watched in horror as he saw what was happening to his friend. He stomped both feet and tossed his head in large circles, swinging his body around to keep Larry away from him as he tried to figure out what he could do to help Marinera. He let out a scream of anger as he felt Larry's pitchfork connect with his own rump, then his neck, and finally he felt it land across his face. He went blind with fury, rearing up, trying to knock the weapon out of the man's grasp so he couldn't use it anymore. As he reared up once more Larry pointed the pitchfork right toward his chest. Gallant didn't care. He was tired of the bullying and the attacks from both Flash and these men. He struck out with his hooves at the weapon, this time moving forward as he did so, forcing Larry to step backward and fall into the dirty straw behind him. He saw the fear in the man's eyes as he looked up at the horse. Gallant knew that this time he had won.

"Stop it! Stop it right now!" he heard Jenny yell through the commotion as she and Albert ran up to their stalls. Ted stopped the attack at the sound of Jenny's voice. Gallant put all four feet back on the ground, looking over to see how Marinera was faring. She stood there shaking uncontrollably. She had never experienced a person being cruel and could not understand what had happened.

Jenny threw open the stall door and grabbed Larry by his shirt, dragging him out. She was small, but she was angry, and strong from handling horses over the years. Albert was already in with Marinera, calming her as Ted lay on the floor in the aisleway where Albert had thrown him. Both men had obviously been drinking heavily and were in no condition to put up much of a fight.

"Albert, lock these two in the tack room until the police arrive. I'm going to make sure they never have the chance to work around animals again," Jenny fumed.

As Albert escorted Ted and Larry to the tack room, Jenny entered Marinera's stall. She stroked her neck, calming her, making sure that she didn't have any cuts or puncture wounds from the pitchfork. It seemed that she would be fine once she had some time to get over the experience. Then she came in to check on Gallant.

"I have a feeling those two may be the reason you are afraid of the whip," she said as she felt along his body and checked his head where the pitchfork had made contact. He had a couple of scrape marks along his rump that she would need to put some wound cream on, but he had come through the ordeal mostly unscathed. Jenny knew that for both horses there would be some psychological scars that would take time to heal.

"I'm sorry that you've seen the ugly side of how people can be, Gallant. Don't let it change who you are. Give the rest of us a chance, okay?" she said softly.

Jenny made sure both horses had fresh hay and water and left to tell the policemen what had happened.

Gallant looked over the partition between their stalls at Marinera.

"Are you okay?" he asked urgently.

She nodded. "I will be. How about you?"

"I knew those men were bad," Gallant said, still angry at what he had witnessed. "I'm so sorry I couldn't help you more, Marinera."

Marinera looked at him, her eyes becoming soft as she understood what he was feeling. "You did everything you could, Gallant. None of this was your fault. Just like what happened with Gracie was no one's fault, and yet you still carry the weight of the guilt. Those men are evil, and I can't believe I didn't see it sooner. Is that why you fear the whip? Did they hurt you when they brought you here?"

Gallant nodded. "I never realized that humans could be so cruel," he responded. "I think I was very lucky that I had only known love and gentleness my whole life until that day. I feel so terrible for horses that have less than that."

Flash had witnessed everything. He knew the men would not have survived the ordeal if they had tried that with him. He had seen how Gallant had held back even through his anger, trying to take out the weapon, not the man. Listening to him and Marinera talk, Flash understood a little more about Gallant's background. The knowledge didn't change anything as far as what he had told Gallant about his physical limitations, but he recognized there may be more to the horse than he first assumed.

"Eat up, Weakling," he said to Gallant. "If you were stronger those men would never have tried to do that to you."

Although it sounded cruel, Flash was giving Gallant what he thought was sound advice: they all prey on the weak. The sooner Gallant understood that, the sooner he could correct the situation. That was as close to being nice as Flash got. He hoped Gallant appreciated it.

*****

After that day, the horses never saw Ted and Larry again and things soon settled back into the usual routine. Gallant cooperated with Jenny during his lessons, learning how to move in each direction at the end of the lunge line, move his shoulder away from pressure, and place his feet where Jenny instructed him to. He took the weight of the saddle and tolerated the feel of the girth tightening around his middle. He obediently opened his mouth to accept the bit and learned how the rider's hands would eventually send him signals through it so he would understand what was being asked of him.

But when the day came for Jenny to step up into the saddle, Gallant decided that was where he would draw the line. What was the point of being ridden if he would never be good enough for anything? So as Jenny put her foot in the stirrup and swung her leg over his back, he laid down, simply laid down in the middle of the arena. He didn't want to risk hurting Jenny, who had shown him nothing but kindness, but he would not allow himself to be ridden by anyone but Gracie either.

Jenny tried again for the next few days, always with the same result. She could see that the young horse was not thriving here. He had been losing weight, and his coat was becoming dull. It was as if he had no drive, no spirit. He had been there for almost six weeks by this time and most horses adjusted to their new surroundings within the first week. It was time to call Harriet and tell her there was nothing more she could do for this horse. She would recommend that Gallant be sold.

Chapter Ten

IN HER MIND,
LOVE WAS EVERYTHING

Harriet put the phone down and turned to her husband with a look of dismay. Roy put down the newspaper he was reading and invited his wife to sit next to him. He had heard Harriet's side of the conversation with Jenny but had not heard the trainer's side of the story.

"So, what was Jenny saying about Gallant?" he queried.

"It didn't sound good." Harriet shook her head sadly. "He doesn't even sound like the same horse we had here," she said. "Jenny said he cooperated in his lessons, but when it came to riding him, he wouldn't even let her get on. He just laid down on the ground and refused to get up again. She has never seen anything like it. She also said that he has lost weight and is obviously not happy. Maybe we should bring him home, Roy. I'm not sure he can handle being away from Gracie."

Roy knew that he was going to have to be the one to make the hard decision. His wife and daughter were both too emotionally involved with their horses, which marred their perspective of the situation they were now facing.

"So, after all this time he's not even been ridden, Harriet? And he's refusing to continue with his training? What would happen if we brought him home? He would be dangerous for Gracie to ride with no training under saddle, and you know that eventually she would be tempted to try and get on him again. We can't risk that. The next time she could be hurt even worse."

Harriet knew that Roy was right. She also knew that Gracie would be devastated if Gallant did not return home. Roy reached for Harriet's hand. "Maybe we could soften the blow somewhat by getting her a nice, safe horse to ride. My brother called today. They are moving from the country to a place in town and they need to find a new home for their two horses, Rick and Jazz. What if we brought them here and put them under Gracie's charge? They are both safe children's horses, and she would be able to ride with her cousins when they come to visit."

"Oh, she would love that!" exclaimed Harriet, cheering at the thought. She knew that Gracie may never be able to replace the bond she had with Gallant, but maybe this would be a place to start the healing. "Do you think we could get her lessons with Jane at her riding school in San Jose?" Harriet asked. "Once the doctors clear her for riding again, of course. I know it's an additional expense, but the better rider she becomes, the less danger she has of having an accident. Jane is so good with her junior riders, and even takes them to endurance competitions. Gracie would love that!'

Roy nodded. "I think that's a good plan. Let's surprise Gracie when she gets home from school one day next week. We can have Rick and Jazz in the paddock that used to be Gallant's. It will help to soften the blow when we tell her the news about him."

With the best plan they could come up with in place, Roy and Harriet hoped their daughter would not react too badly when she heard Gallant was being sold. At least she'd had several weeks to get used to him not being at the ranch, and the new horses would keep her mind and hands busy while she adjusted to the news.

*****

Gracie was back at school now, although there were only a couple of weeks left before the summer break began. She and Fling had become even closer during her recovery, and as usual he was at the end of the long driveway waiting for her as she got off the school bus at the end of the day. Once he saw Gracie he bounced up and down with joy, barking his welcome as she pet his head in greeting. They started their walk down the long driveway and past the pear orchards to the ranch house and stables. Gracie still had the special boot on for now, instead of the cast, although when she was at home she hardly used it anymore.

She looked up as she approached the stable area to see her parents waiting for her by the barn. *Gallant must be home!* she thought, and wished she were able to run the rest of the way to see him. She hoped and prayed that nothing would have changed between them. But, instead of Gallant, Gracie spotted two strange horses grazing in Gallant's paddock, their heads lifting in unison as she approached. On closer inspection, they were not strange at all. They were the horses from her cousins' house, Rick and Jazz.

Gracie finally reached her parents and looked at them quizzically. Where were her cousins? Were they here visiting? Her parents had made no mention of them coming here this morning before she left for school. Roy and Harriet were both looking at Gracie, her father smiling broadly, her mother a little less so.

"What are Rick and Jazz doing here, Mother?" Gracie asked.

Her mother rested her hands on Gracie's shoulders and turned her toward her father. "Your father has something to tell you, Gracie," she said.

Gracie looked at her father, wondering what could possibly be going on. For a moment she had thought that Gallant might be home, and the sudden hope she had experienced had now been replaced with a deep clenching of her stomach, and a strange feeling that things were about to change.

"Gracie," Roy began, "Your aunt, uncle and cousins have moved into town now and needed a new home for

Rick and Jazz. They agreed that they could come and live here, to be in your care. It's a big responsibility for a little girl, but once the doctor clears you to ride, you will have two safe horses that will take care of you on your riding adventures. Your mother and I have also agreed to get you some lessons with Jane in San Jose once a week, so you can learn to ride properly. The thing is, Gracie, Gallant has not done well with his training. He's not safe for you to ride, or even for your mother. We've had to let him go to a new home."

As her father spoke, Gracie's mind slowly absorbed his words. Gallant would not be coming back. Ever. Her worst nightmare was coming true. Gracie would never again be able to feel his heartbeat as she lay resting with him in his stall. She would never again be able to share all her secrets with him, or cry into his mane when she was unhappy. The most important friend she'd ever had would be out of reach, living somewhere without her, and worst of all, never knowing that she didn't blame him for what had happened. Gracie felt her legs begin to buckle underneath her. She tried to smile up at her parents so they wouldn't see how much pain she was in, but the world closed in around her and became black. She thankfully slipped into a place where she just didn't hurt anymore.

*****

When Gracie came to, she was lying on the couch in the living room. Her mother handed her a glass of water and she took a sip. Slowly she remembered why she was there. Gallant was never coming home. He had been sold and she would probably never even know where he had gone. To her, this was almost worse than if he had died, because she would constantly worry about the pain he was in being away from her. She would wonder if he truly knew how much she loved him and if he knew the accident had been *her* fault, not his. She wondered if even her mother knew the extent of what she had lost.

"I'm sorry for passing out, Mother. It was such a shock," she said quietly. She looked around her. "Where's Daddy?"

"I asked him to wait outside, to give us a few minutes alone, Gracie," Harriet answered. "I know hearing that Gallant is not coming home was a huge shock to you. I, as much as anyone, understand your connection to him. I was there from the beginning, remember?"

Gracie nodded her head. The night of Gallant's birth was as clear in her mind now as it had been five years ago.

"But you need to understand that sometimes in a relationship with a horse love just isn't enough. Imagine if Gallant came home but he was never ridden. It wouldn't be fair to him. He needs to be with someone who can give him a job, where he can become a real horse and not just a pet. He deserves that, Gracie. Sometimes when we really love someone, we must let them go, so they can live the life they were meant to live."

Julie tried to process what her mother was saying. She had never for a moment considered that the most perfect place for Gallant was not with her. In her mind, love was everything.

"Your father loves you, Gracie," Harriet was saying. "He loves you so much that he's not willing to put you in harm's way again and risk having Gallant here. He loves you so much that he has bought you two new horses that will take care of you when you ride them, and that you can enjoy for years to come. He has also agreed to let you have riding lessons every weekend with Jane at her stables, where you can meet other girls your age that love horses as much as you do. Do you think you can find it in your heart to try and understand what we had to do?"

Gracie heard her mother's words, and knew that once the pain receded, if it ever did, she was sure she would be able to see the truth in them.

"Mother, have you ever lost anything that left you feeling like you were so empty your heart was struggling to beat?"

Harriet nodded. "I have, Gracie, and I need you to trust me when I say you will heal. Your life may never be exactly the same, but you will find a way to navigate through this, and you will come out the other side. A good friend reminded me once that within every day there is a best moment, we just have to find it. If you move forward looking for that moment in each day, it will remind you that you still have many blessings in your life to be thankful for. I know Rick and Jazz won't replace Gallant, nothing ever will, but they are a good place to start the healing, right?"

Gracie listened to her mother talk and realized that what was done was done. Her father had brought two new horses here. Two horses that she could ride and care for.

She got off the couch and opened the door to the living room where her father was pacing nervously outside. She hugged her father tightly, then reached her arms toward her mother to include her in the embrace.

Gracie pulled back and looked up at both her parents. "Thank you" she said simply, knowing that from now on she would only mourn Gallant in private.

"I love my new horses already. May I go outside and see them now?"

"Of course, Gracie," Harriet said, looking over her daughter's head at her husband. "Why don't you and Fling go across to the stables and get to know your new horses a little better. They could do with a good grooming after their trip here today."

Gracie headed slowly over to the barn to get the grooming items she would need and both the horse's halters. She wondered if she would ever get used to not seeing Gallant running toward her in his paddock. No horse could ever replace him, but she would try to enjoy these new horses and give them the love and care they deserved.

Before she went to greet Rick and Jazz, Gracie stopped by Magri's stall. The mare came to her, used to the daily visits since she and Gracie had bonded after Gallant's departure. As she got closer, she could tell that something was wrong. Gracie was looking at her strangely and struggling to find her words. Magri reached her and put her muzzle close to Gracie's face, trying to figure out what was happening.

"Oh, Magri," Gracie said, tears starting to pour down her cheeks. "He's gone, Magri. Gallant is gone forever."

Chapter Eleven

IN THAT MOMENT, A PACT WAS MADE

Gallant knew that something was different. A couple of times this week he had been taken out of his pen, bathed and groomed, and led into the arena where strangers watched him being lunged in circles in both directions. Then they would run their hands up and down his legs, usually shaking their heads, and eventually Gallant would be returned to his stall to wait for the next time this would happen.

One day, a boy poked his head over the stall gate and stood there looking at Gallant, staring at him intently. He must have been around twelve years old and had that gawky awkwardness of a boy about to enter his teenage years. His mousy brown hair was tousled and messy and as he stood there, he took large bites out of a juicy green pear.

Gallant looked at him suspiciously. He sensed that this human was similar to Gracie in that he was not fully grown yet, but Gallant had become distrustful of strangers since his life had changed so much in the last few weeks. He watched the boy finish eating the pear, and then hold his hand out flat toward the horse, the core resting temptingly in his palm. He had a kind look in his eyes and a gentle presence. Gallant took a tentative step toward him. Could he trust this person? In his heart he was desperate to make a connection with a human again. It had been weeks since he had seen Gracie, and he missed the time they had spent together. The smell of the pear reminded him of home, of the rows of trees in the orchards and the many times he and Gracie had sat beneath them, content to be in each other's company.

Gallant licked his lips and moved his jaw, taking another step closer. The core was now within reach and he grabbed it quickly, careful not to hurt the boy's skin with his teeth. He savored the sweet taste of the pear as he chewed it, the sticky juices seeping into the corners of his mouth. He nodded his head approvingly, and the boy laughed.

Jenny appeared behind the boy then, looking sadly at Gallant. It was a look that she often had on her face when she was around him, and Gallant knew that he had disappointed her. He hadn't done it intentionally, he just couldn't live up to what she expected of him.

The boy turned. "Who is this horse, Aunt Jenny? He's an Arabian, isn't he?"

Jenny stood behind her nephew, her hands on his shoulders. He had grown since last summer and now the top of his head was almost to her chin.

"Yes, Jack, he is an Arabian. He came here about three months ago, but I'm afraid I haven't had much success with him. His owners have agreed to sell him, but I haven't managed to find a buyer yet. He's learned all his groundwork, but he just won't let me get on his back. He doesn't buck or rear, he just lays down. I know there must be something in his past that is causing this. He obviously doesn't want to hurt me, but frankly, I can't keep taking the owners' money to train a horse that doesn't appear trainable."

Jenny looked at Gallant, running her eyes over him. "His conformation isn't perfect, but there's something different about him and my gut tells me this horse has something special. I am just completely stumped at how to bring it out of him."

Jack looked at the Arabian who was watching them both intently.

"Can I try riding him?" he asked. "I can sense that this horse could learn to trust me. I just need to figure him out."

Jenny thought for a moment. The horse had never done anything dangerous. She knew that he had been very bonded to a young girl at his former home, so maybe he would find it easier to trust her nephew. Jack had grown up riding, spending time every summer at Greenhill Training Stables, helping his aunt care for the horses in return for riding lessons. Jack had a natural seat. He was balanced and could read a horse's movements well. His hands were gentle but firm, using only the amount of pressure necessary to help the horse understand what he was asking of it. Jenny trusted her nephew's natural horse sense, as well as his ability to bring out the best in the animals he worked with, even at such a young age. At twelve, his parents had released him to her for the whole summer, so there would be three months where he and Gallant could work together. It may be the best chance the young horse had, possibly the only one.

"Let me call his owners and talk to them," Jenny told her nephew. "Maybe if I offer to keep him here at no cost, with you working with him, they'll agree to hold off selling him until the end of the summer when hopefully he can actually be ridden. It will certainly make him easier to sell. In the meantime, why don't you start spending time with him every day. His name is Gallant, and I think he could really use a friend."

Jack loved a challenge, and he was also very drawn to this young horse with sad eyes who looked like he had a story to tell, if Jack could only figure it out.

"Can I take him out of his stall for a walk around?" he asked Jenny, who nodded and handed him the red halter hanging outside the stall door.

Gallant eyed Jack nervously as he entered the stall. Jack approached him slowly, moving past his head and standing quietly at his shoulder. When Gallant didn't move away, Jack stroked the horse's neck with the back of his hand, talking to him in a low murmur, reassuring him that he was safe. Gallant relaxed, turning his head toward the boy, a silent agreement between them that he would accept the halter in the boy's hands. Jack gently slipped it over Gallant's nose and secured it behind his ears. He didn't lead him out of the stall right away, but instead ran his hands over Gallant's body, pausing if he sensed any tension in the horse.

"There, boy," Jack murmured. Then he continued, talking as much to himself as the horse. "Your pasterns are a bit long, but your legs are tight and firm, and I can't feel any sign of splint or tendon issues."

Jack knew that the horse hadn't ever been ridden and that had allowed his bones to grow without the stress of weight on his back. All these factors could offset the fact that his natural shape was not ideal, and besides, it was often a horse's mind that was the deciding factor in whether a horse was successful or not in whatever job he was destined to do.

Jack's hands continued traveling over the horse, passing across his rump, and running down his back legs towards his hocks.

"Your back legs are upright, and that could make for a bumpy ride for me, but we won't find out if there's any loss of power until we take you on some hills."

Jack noticed that Gallant still had a good amount of muscle on his rump, despite a diminished amount of food and only limited exercise over the past couple of weeks. He imagined that if the horse would eat well, and if he would accept the weight of a rider, his back end could be built up to where power may not be an issue.

"Who knows what you could be in a couple of years, Gallant? You're the perfect age to start training for endurance. We just need to get you comfortable under saddle and conditioned. You're a good-looking boy and could make someone a wonderful horse."

Gallant had a nice eye once he relaxed and was no longer nervous. His dark mane and tail contrasted against the deep red of his bay coat, the crooked white blaze running from forehead to muzzle standing out against the rest of his face. Jack was right, he had the promise of being a good-looking horse as he finished maturing.

Gallant sensed that this boy was truly seeing him. He didn't feel like he was being criticized like he had when those other people came to see him. Gallant's confidence had been shattered when he had been taken away from his home in the Valley of Heart's Delight. He had felt embarrassed and worthless since he had come here, especially with the negative comments from Flash, a horse he secretly admired. He had felt lost in this new world. Gallant knew that Gracie had loved him without question, that she would have loved and accepted him with all his flaws regardless of what they were. But here was a boy, a stranger, who could obviously see something in Gallant at this first meeting, knowing nothing about him other than what he saw, and sensed.

"We could really learn to like each other if you would give me a chance," Jack said, resting his hand on Gallant's neck, before reaching down to stroke the soft spot at the side of his muzzle. "I think you were meant for great things" he murmured. "You just need to believe in yourself."

Gallant's heart expanded in his chest. He may not have understood the boy's words exactly, but he understood what he was saying. All the sadness he had been holding inside was released in a big sigh. Gallant gave the boy a look that said, *I'm ready to trust again. Let me show you what I can do.* A silent understanding passed between boy and horse. Jack nodded his head, picked up the lead rope, and led Gallant out of the stall.

Together they exited the barn and meandered over to a grassy area with trees dotted around, providing shade for them to stand while Gallant munched on the sweet green grass. This was the first time he had been outside of the barn since his arrival, other than in the run attached to his stall. The smell of the fresh air and sight of the mountains in the distance allowed his soul to breathe. He could finally see to a horizon again, just like he'd been able to at home. The scenery was different, but his appreciation of it was the same.

The boy did not ask much of him, just moved his feet to new ground every minute or so and then allowed him to continue eating. Every now and then he would reach over and scratch him on the neck until he found a spot that Gallant particularly liked, at which point Jack would laugh as Gallant demanded more of the same. After ten minutes or so, Jack signaled to him that they were going to start moving again and began walking him along the dirt lane that looped around the barn area. Gallant passed new sights he'd not been able to see from his paddock. If something concerned him, he would hesitate, and the boy would come to a standstill, not forcing the young horse to move toward anything he felt scared of, but waiting until Gallant was ready to move past the strange object when he realized there was no danger. The only time he spooked was when a wild turkey flew out of the brush to his right, making him jump sideways. When he realized where the noise had come from, he looked at Jack to see if he was upset with him for spooking, but Jack just laughed and patted him on the neck.

"It's okay, Gallant! That made me jump as well!" he reassured him.

The boy and the horse kept walking until they had made their way around the perimeter of the barn. Some of the horses in their stalls ventured outside when they heard the muted noise of Gallant's hooves on the dirt. When they saw who it was, many of them whinnied, happy to see he was getting some attention and looking much happier than he had since his arrival. Many of them had witnessed how Gallant had dealt with Larry and Ted's attack and they were grateful to him for getting those men away from the stables once and for all.

"Look at you, Gallant!" one of them neighed loudly. "It's good to see you out enjoying yourself for once! It's about time you had some fun!"

Gallant walked even taller after realizing the other horses were watching him. Maybe things might really turn around for him.

Once Jack had led Gallant around two whole loops of the barn, and Gallant was relaxed with all the new sights and smells he encountered, Jack found a fallen log and sat down on it. Keeping Gallant's head turned toward him, he began talking to the horse gently.

"Good job, fella," he began. "I know that something has scared you, and that you have been really sad. Maybe you're just homesick. I know I was the first summer I came to stay with Aunt Jenny without my parents. But here's the thing. You need to let me ride you. I can teach you so many things you need to know this summer. A horse that is smart and understands how humans communicate with them have a much better life than those who don't."

Jack reached up, stroking Gallant's face.

"I don't know your whole story, Gallant, but I promise you this. I will never ask more of you than you are prepared to give. If you trust me, I will keep you safe, and if you will allow me to be your friend, I will fight for you when the time comes for you to go to a new home, and I will make sure that it will be a good one for you. Do you think you can trust me enough to ride you?"

Gallant knew that the boy was offering his friendship, and he felt like he could trust this new person, at least until he found Gracie again. Now he was thinking more rationally, Gallant realized that he had been going about this all wrong. He should have been welcoming the lessons and learning as much as he could, so that when Gracie found him, he would know exactly how to take care of her properly and be able to move confidently beneath her like he had seen Flash moving with Jenny. He had been letting his guilt since the accident cloud his judgement. This new person was offering him a second chance to do the right thing, and he wasn't going to mess this up again. He lowered his head, resting it on the boy's shoulder. Jack leaned in toward his muzzle, the boy and the horse's breath mingling in the stillness they found together. In that moment, a pact was made.

Gallant turned his body sideways to the boy as Jack stood up. Jack looked at him for a moment, surprised, but certain that he understood what Gallant was offering. He fastened the lead rope to each side of the halter and placed it gently over Gallant's head. Then he took a step back and upwards onto the fallen tree trunk where he had been sitting. Gallant stepped closer to the boy, his back level with Jack's torso. Jack ran his hand along Gallant's back and then gently leaned his body across the horse. He needed to make sure that Gallant would be accepting of his weight before taking this exercise any further. Gallant stood still, but relaxed. He felt the warmth of the boy's body covering his. It was not an unpleasant feeling. Without the saddle strapped to his back there was direct contact between Jack and the horse, and each could feel the other's lungs expanding with each breath, feel every flicker of movement where they were connected.

Very slowly, Jack leaned forward over Gallant's neck, petting him, running his hands over any part of the horse's body he could reach. When he was sure the horse was ready, he lifted his leg over Gallant's back, being careful not to drag it over his rump, and allowed it to settle on the other side. He lowered himself down gently until he was sitting astride the horse while maintaining contact with him evenly, from his hip through his ankle. Gallant was careful not to move, not wanting to let the boy fall, as Gracie had done. Gallant had seen Jenny riding the other horses in the arena. He had seen Gracie riding Andy and Harriet riding Magri, and now that he was thinking clearly, he understood that people didn't often fall or get hurt, so he tried to stay relaxed and pay attention to what Jack was asking of him.

Jack began to repeat certain words to him. Jenny had also used specific words during his groundwork training so he understood some of what Jack was saying. He needed to make the connection between the words and what he felt Jack doing on his back. At the same time as Jack used the word "walk" he felt the boy's legs squeeze ever so gently against his sides. Gallant took a tentative step. Was this what the boy was asking him to do? Jack petted his neck, offering words of encouragement. The next time Jack squeezed his legs, Gallant took three steps forward, and then hesitated again, until the legs squeezed again and held that feeling as Gallant began moving forward at a walk, following the direction Jack was guiding his head, just like when he was being led.

By the time Jenny came back down to the barn she was astonished to see Jack sitting astride Gallant, gently turning him in figure eight circles, bareback, with only a halter and lead rope. The horse looked relaxed and happy, one ear cocked back toward his rider, focusing on every sound and movement the boy was making. Jenny knew she should be mad at Jack for not waiting until she was there to try and mount the horse in case something had gone wrong, but seeing the success that Jack was already having with Gallant it was hard to be upset with him. Jenny walked over and took hold of Gallant's halter.

"I don't know how you did it, Jack, but I have to say that is a sight I never thought I would see!"

Jack patted Gallant one more time, and then gently threw his leg back over the horse's rump and slid to the ground. He wrapped his arms around Gallant's neck, knowing that he had just received a huge gift of trust from the young horse, and kissed him on the side of his soft muzzle.

Jenny watched the interaction between boy and horse. "I think, based on this, you will be very happy to know that I have spoken to Gallant's owner, who has agreed to let you work with him this summer while you're here."

Jack's eyes shone at the news. He looked at Gallant and saw the same light reflected in the horse's eyes. It

seemed that both boy and horse had found the perfect way to spend the warm, summer days at Greenhill
Training Stables. Neither could wait for the next training
session to begin.

Chapter Twelve

BALANCE AND TENACITY

Gracie's life was beginning to find a new rhythm. While she still missed Gallant, and always would, the two new horses that came into her life each offered her comfort in their own way. At least twice a week she would hop bareback on Jazz and go for a leisurely stroll through the tall mustard grass that bloomed every spring at the ranch. Since Jazz was older and couldn't tolerate being ridden too far, Gracie would often hop off the horse and hand walk him, decorating his long mane with fronds from the pampas grass she found along their route.

The doctor had cleared her to ride again, so every weekend her mother would trailer her and Rick over to Jane's stables where Gracie took an hour of riding lessons. After the first few weeks Jane suggested that Harriet leave Gracie at the stables all day. In return for doing some easy chores, Gracie could go out on the longer trail rides with a group of young girls known as Jane's Juniors. Jane was very involved with the sport of endurance riding and was happy to introduce young people to the sport by teaching them the basics and offering group rides over increasingly long distances. Some of the children had their own horses, and others borrowed horses from Jane's stable. The children ranged in age from nine to sixteen and were at various skill levels, depending on how long they'd been riding.

Gracie found that her romps around the orchards with her pony had given her a great deal of experience when it came to the balance and tenacity it took to be a successful endurance rider. Covering rough ground at a fast trot over varying terrain required balance and skill. The trails were a constant challenge to both horse and rider. Low hanging branches could sweep an unsuspecting rider off their horse, and streams and rivers could pose a problem for horses that had never left a stable yard before.

Rick was the perfect starter horse for Gracie in the sport. Even though he could be a little lazy at the outset, once he got going he was happy to maintain a good speed. He would go through any kind of water obstacle, pop easily over fallen tree branches laying across the trail and didn't pin his ears back or threaten other horses in the group. Even though Gracie was one of the youngest girls at ten years old, Jane recognized that she was one of the most talented riders she had mentored in a while. She decided to talk to Harriet about taking Gracie to an actual endurance ride later that summer. She wanted to see if Harriet was on board with the idea before bringing the subject up to Gracie herself, just in case her parents had any reservations.

When Harriet arrived to pick up her daughter that evening, Jane pulled her aside while the Juniors finished sweeping out the barn.

"Gracie is an incredibly talented girl," she began. "Her ankle doesn't appear to be bothering her when she's riding so I'd like to take her on some even longer rides if that's okay with you and her father. In fact, I think she'd make a great member of our junior endurance team if that's something you'd consider."

Harriet was excited for Gracie, but she needed to make sure the idea was favorable to Roy before agreeing to anything. It was one thing to lose his daughter for a day to the local stables, but Harriet knew that often endurance rides could take up an entire weekend, or longer. Jane didn't often take her Juniors out of state but tried to stick to the more local rides, although those could be several hours away.

"Could you give me an idea of the costs involved, Jane. Roy will want to know before we can make a decision."

Jane understood that costs could be a concern, so every year she held several fundraisers in the community so every child on the team would have the same opportunity to participate.

"It's actually not too bad," she explained to Harriet. "Gracie already has a suitable horse for the limited distance rides, which are generally twenty-five miles. She can use her current tack for that distance, so really it's just the entry fee for the ride and food for the weekend. She would need to bring a sleeping bag and a backpack, her riding gear and a few changes of clothing. Junior ride fees are usually a lot less than the adult fee, and we only attend one ride a month, mostly during the times that the children are out of school. There's a couple of local ones that might be during the school semester but those would be very close by."

Harriet nodded. She knew without a doubt that this would be something Gracie would want to do. She would have to talk to Roy this evening and see if he would agree to at least let Gracie give it a try.

"One other thing," Jane added. "Some of these children become extremely enamored with this sport and want to move up to the fifty-mile rides. If Gracie wants to do that, she might need a different horse, and more specialized tack. It wouldn't be fair to ask Rick to go beyond his abilities, and besides, he'd get pulled at the vet check if he wasn't doing well. I'm just giving you fair warning because I can already see how determined Gracie is, and how much she loves being around the horses. I could see her going far in this sport."

"Thank you, Jane," Harriet replied. "I think you're right that Gracie could very well become obsessed with endurance! There's nothing she enjoys more than being around her horses."

On their way home, Gracie chattered endlessly about her day at the stables, and how well Rick had done on that day's seven-mile ride.

"We trotted a lot, Mother," she said excitedly. "Rick jumped over this huge log that had fallen across the trail, and then we went over a wooden bridge that crossed the river! Did you even know there was such a thing as an endurance ride? Jane knows some people who have done a hundred miles on their horses in a big race up in the Sierra mountains, and she's done lots of fifty-mile races herself. She says there are rides all over the country, and even in other countries. You can camp with your horses and sleep near them all night, and I would be able to hang out with all my new friends. I think Rick would love it too, and you could come and ride as well, or you could help in camp."

Gracie had to take a breath. She had never talked so fast in her life, but she couldn't get the thoughts in her brain out of her mouth fast enough.

"Wow, slow down, Gracie. That's an awful lot of information to absorb," her mother said, laughing. "Let me talk to your father about it. It's a huge time commitment, and while the costs aren't too bad right now, I can see them adding up in the future. But you're a good student and I think if you keep your grades up while you're doing this, he won't have too much of a problem with it."

Gracie hoped her mother was right. When they pulled up to their barn she unloaded her horse from the trailer, brushed him one more time, and put him away in his stall where he was greeted by Jazz who was always enthusiastic to see his stable mate after he had been gone all day. Gracie made sure that both horses had plenty of hay and water for the night, and then, happy but exhausted, she went inside to have her own dinner and await the decision her parents would be making about her future.

Chapter Thirteen

THE OPPORTUNITY TO SOAR

Jenny made sure to be there assisting Jack and Gallant the first few times they worked in the arena. She showed Jack the groundwork training they had done, and they found a comfortable saddle for Jack that fit Gallant's back correctly.

"You'll have to keep an eye on that saddle fit over the next few weeks," Jenny warned her nephew.

"As Gallant becomes fitter his shape will change and we may need to switch him into a different saddle."

"I can't wait to see how Gallant looks with some additional weight and muscle," Jack enthused.

The first time Jack got on Gallant in the arena he could tell the horse was trying hard, but it was all so new for him. The feel of the rider in the saddle, rather than being ridden bareback was quite different, and Gallant had to learn to balance through the turns, all the while staying within the pace that his rider set for him. He learned quickly, and after the first couple of weeks was able to do all the basics: walk, trot, canter in a circle, move and stop at the cues given by the rider's seat and hands. He was even trotting over ground poles.

Jack could not have been more pleased with Gallant. As a reward after the lessons, Jack would strip the horse of his tack, hose the sweat off his body and take him outside to eat the abundant grass under the trees while his coat dried.

Gallant ate voraciously now that he was no longer depressed. He also knew that in order to look anything like Flash he had to eat all that was put in front of him, and drink plenty of water. He couldn't wait for the day that Jack would take him out on the trails so they could ride across the foothills of the ranch together. As it turned out, he didn't have to wait long.

One morning, Jenny asked Jack if he wanted to bring Gallant along with her and Flash while they did an easy five-mile workout. Gallant laughed at the look on Flash's face when they were tacked up and led outside together. Since the day Flash had told him he had no hope of ever being an endurance horse, the two had barely spoken. Gallant no longer stood in the corner of his stall with his head hung low. He moved proudly, knowing he was doing well in his lessons and that Jack was pleased with him. Unlike Flash, Marinera had been nothing but encouraging and supportive, telling Gallant every day how well he was doing in the arena, and how far he had come in such a short time. Gallant realized that he didn't need to be friends with someone like Flash, who was always so negative and intentionally tried to make those around him feel bad. Flash didn't care about anyone except himself, and Gallant actually felt sorry for him now, because Flash would never know how special a bond with a human could be, like he'd had with Gracie, and now with Jack.

The horses were led to a mounting block where Jenny mounted Flash first, gathering up her reins and moving out of the way. Once they were both on their horses, Jenny instructed Jack to always stay several feet behind her so the more experienced horse could show the younger one how to move down the trail, watching his footing and pacing himself according to the ever-changing terrain.

They left the ranch at a walk, and Gallant fell in behind Flash, keeping the same pace and staying a respectful distance behind him. Gallant loved going down the trail. The birds scattered ahead of them, causing the canopy of leaves to drop their morning dew onto the riders and their horses. There were boulders off to the side of the trail in some places, and the footing changed constantly, sometimes firm, sometimes rocky, and occasionally they would come to patches of deep sand where the horses' feet sunk into the soft ground and it took more work to take the next step. When they came to a trail with good footing that wound through some aspens, Jenny asked Flash to move up to a trot. Flash complied and Gallant followed, happy to move with a little more speed. Jack checked in with him often, using his body and words to ask the horse to slow a little, or encouraging him to pick it up. Jack was a very balanced rider and soon he and Gallant found their rhythm. Gallant could feel Jack smiling, and knew the boy was enjoying this as much as he was.

Once they slowed to a walk again, Jack asked his aunt if Gallant could take the lead, just for a moment. Gallant hadn't spooked at all and seemed to naturally enjoy the trail. Jack wanted to see how he felt when he was in front.

"You can take the lead for a few minutes, Jack," Jenny agreed. "It will be good for Flash to follow another horse, but we don't want to ask too much of Gallant his first time out."

Jenny was also interested to observe the young horse and see how he moved down the trail. She was curious if his conformational issues would affect his movement. So far, she had not seen anything of concern in the arena, but the trail demanded a very different skill set so the horse wouldn't trip and fall, potentially hurting himself and his rider.

Gallant happily took the lead.

"Don't think you're something special just because you get a turn in the front, Upstart!" Flash grumbled as he went by.

For a few moments they just walked. Jenny noticed that Gallant's ears were forward, showing interest in what he was doing, but he was relaxed and calm, not overly excited as some young horses could be when they first got out on the trail. Gallant's right ear would flick back toward Jack if the boy spoke to him, showing he was listening and focused on his rider. When Jack asked him to pick his pace up into a trot, he transitioned smoothly from one gait to the other, and Jenny realized with amazement that it was at a trot that Gallant really shone. His feet seemed to glide over the ground, his body leaning into the turns, all the while keeping his rider centered above him. If he came across a fallen branch, he popped over it effortlessly, stepping around any large rocks that could potentially bruise the soles of his hooves. In short, Gallant was a natural on the trail, and he obviously loved it.

"Easy there," Flash called from behind. "You could fall at any second at this speed, taking your rider down with you," he warned.

Gallant just laughed. "If you complain too much, I might think it's because you can't keep up!" he answered. He had a new-found confidence now, and even Flash taunting him with his old fears would not affect him today.

Gallant felt like he was floating. He could feel the trail calling to him. What was around the next bend? When would the footing change again, or a fallen branch offer him the opportunity to soar? Although he had followed Gracie out on the trails back home, being ridden was a different experience. It was a partnership, a union of human and beast. He could *feel* Jack's excitement as they flew along the trail together. He couldn't believe he had been missing out on this for so long! The smells, the sights, even the sounds were intoxicating to him. *This* was adventure. *This* was what had been missing, and what he had been craving for. Gallant had found his passion. He could do this forever.

Jenny called ahead for Jack to pull up at the next opportunity, and when he stopped, she asked Flash to walk up alongside the other horse. Jack's face was lit up with excitement.

"Did you see him, Aunt Jenny!" he said excitedly. "He just glides down the trail effortlessly. He listened to everything I asked of him, and he is so smooth, and so much fun to ride."

While Flash moved with power and purpose, Jenny could see that Gallant moved with lightness and grace. That type of movement was a joy for the rider, and easier on the horse over an accumulation of many miles.

"It's too early to tell just yet," Jenny cautioned. "But from what I've seen so far, Gallant has the potential to be an endurance horse, and a good one at that."

While Gallant could tell the humans were pleased with his performance, he knew that Flash was not happy. Flash could not understand how this scrawny horse could make moving down the trail look so effortless. Flash had to concentrate hard on the trail in front of him, not letting his natural power overtake his skill level. He could certainly carry a lot more weight than Gallant, being a much larger and more powerful horse, but he knew that under a lighter rider Gallant had a chance of doing well. He would never admit he had been wrong, and he would certainly not encourage Gallant in his efforts. Instead, he would watch to see where his weaknesses lay, and make sure that he pointed them out so the other horse would begin to doubt himself again. Flash would take out his competition any way he could.

The group walked back to the barn and both horses were hosed off and put back into their stalls with some supplements and grain. Gallant could hardly wait to tell Marinera what had happened. He was so excited to have finally found his passion, his job, and he knew that Gracie would love to ride him out on the trails if he could ever find her again. In the meantime, he would work hard and learn how to go farther and faster, until the day came where he hoped he could compete against other horses in an endurance competition and see how he stacked up against them. Only then would he know whether he had any real talent for this. He hoped that Jack was as excited as he was to keep training.

Flash refused to speak to Gallant after that day. He had been convinced the other horse was a loser, someone not worth bothering with, but his performance today made him wonder if he was wrong. He saw how Gallant floated down the trail, winding through the forest as if he had been doing it all his life. When they had stopped, Flash had to catch his breath, lungs heaving from the pace Gallant had set, while the other horse still seemed fresh and ready to go again. Flash had been training up to twenty miles a day, several days a week, and should have been far fitter than Gallant, who had spent most of his time sulking in his stall. What would Gallant be like after he had put in some serious training miles?

Flash became angry at the thought. He had been bred to be an endurance star. His sire was a champion in endurance races all over the country. This was the only thing Flash knew how to do, and he expected to be the best at it. He looked over to see Gallant looking at him and lifted his lip in a snarl.

"Don't think you have talent, Upstart, just because you didn't trip on a tree root on your first day. There's a lot more to endurance than you know. I am far superior to you in size and strength, and I have been bred for this. Don't even think you can compete against me."

Gallant looked over at Flash calmly.

"I agree you have me beat in size and strength, Flash, but I think I may have you beat in speed. And it is a race, after all, is it not?"

Flash turned away from Gallant so all the other horse could see was his rump. It was the ultimate sign of disrespect but Gallant no longer cared what Flash thought. He had people who believed in him now, and more importantly, he was beginning to believe in himself. For the first time since he had arrived, he was excited about his future.

PART TWO

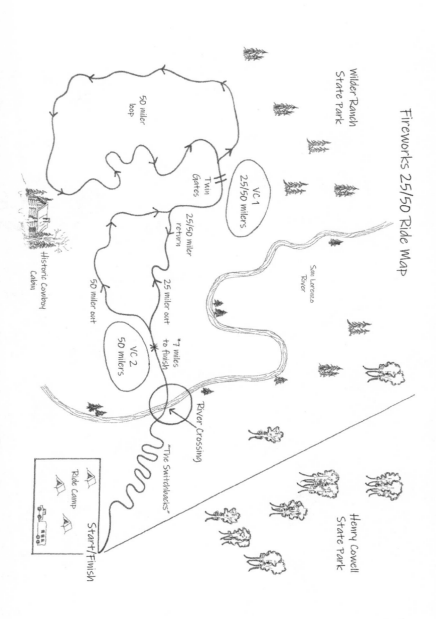

Fireworks 25/50 Ride Map

Chapter Fourteen

HIS NAME IS JOSHUA

Gracie would be thirteen next month. She was no longer a little girl. She still adored her parents and loved being at home in the Valley of Heart's Delight, but she also enjoyed her independence, especially going to the endurance rides with Jane and all the other Juniors. It was the first time she had friends who were as horse crazy as she was. She could spend whole weekends with the horses and with her best friends, April and Penny.

She had met them both when she'd started her riding lessons at Jane's. She had been immediately accepted into the group of girls, mostly because they were just like her.

April rode a quarter horse named Milarky. She was very quiet and kept to herself, too shy to gossip and chatter with the other girls at the stables. But one day out on the trail, Milarky had refused to cross the stream near the beginning of their training ride. It had rained hard overnight, and the normally placid stream had swollen to four times its usual width. Although it was only about a foot deep, its surface was broken by ripples and shadows and Milarky was very unsure whether he wanted to risk putting his feet in there, even though the others had already crossed safely to the other side.

Gracie had been watching the girl and the horse struggle with the day's conditions ever since they had left the parking lot. She was sorry they were having such a hard time, so she quickly took Rick back across the river and brought him alongside April and Milarky on the other side of the bank.

"It's not as bad as it looks, April," she said to the girl, whose teeth were now chattering with the cold. "Did you see as I crossed that the water was hardly above Rick's pasterns? The creek is a lot wider than usual but not really any deeper. Once Milarky realizes that he will be fine! Why don't you ride him right next to Rick's shoulder so he feels safe, and I'll grab his reins for a second to keep him next to me until his feet are in the water and he can see there's no danger."

April nodded gratefully to Gracie and made sure that Milarky stayed right next to Rick as they entered the water. Just as Gracie had predicted, once Milarky felt the ground just beneath the shallow water and realized there was nothing to be fearful of, he splashed right across.

"I'll bet on the way back he'll go right in all by himself," Gracie said, smiling at April.

From that moment on they were fast friends.

*****

Gracie was admired at the barn not only because of her excellent riding skills and passion for the horses, but also because she was kind and helpful. She was mature for her age, and although she enjoyed the bantering back and forth between the girls, she was very focused on becoming the best endurance rider she could be, and that meant putting in a lot of hours in the saddle.

Her other close friend, Penny, who was a year older than her, was a girl who had been obsessed with horses her whole life. She didn't have one of her own, but she'd read every book about horses she could lay her hands on. Penny and Gracie had spent many hours on the trail discussing the merits of their favorite books like *Black Beauty* and *National Velvet*. When they trained at speed, allowing their horses to break into a hand gallop on a wide, flat piece of trail, they both imagined they were riding The Pie in the Grand Nationals, the only girl among a field of male jockeys soaring toward the finish line for a spectacular win!

Penny was riding one of Jane's retired endurance horses who had completed many rides. He was seventeen now, but Jasper still had plenty of miles left in him and was perfect for carrying a lightweight junior rider. One evening Jane's junior team were sitting around at the barn planning their next endurance race. There was a local ride approaching that was both challenging and had stunning scenery. It was called the Fireworks 50. It started in Santa Cruz and the trail took the riders through miles of redwood trees and open meadows, and even passed views of the ocean. There was quite a significant river crossing, but there would be volunteers to supervise that part of the ride, and on a hot day, the river was a great place for the horses to cool off. Jane thought the girls would be able to handle it just fine.

"Can I do the fifty mile ride this time?" Penny asked Jane. "I know Jasper could do it." Jane agreed. Penny and

Jasper had enough twenty-five miles rides behind them to know how everything worked. They were used to following the marker ribbons on the trail and experienced at how to get through the vet checks.

"April, you and Milarky can do the twenty-five-mile ride with Gracie and Rick, although I'm afraid you'll have to take it slowly as Rick is getting older and it's quite a challenging trail," Jane pointed out.

As Jane had predicted, after Gracie had competed in a few twenty-five-mile limited distance competitions on Rick, it became clear that although his heart was in it, his size and breeding were not ideal for endurance. Rick was now well past his prime and shouldn't be pushed beyond his limits.

"Sorry, April," Gracie said. "I can't go any faster than Rick is comfortable going. I'll help you with the river crossing though!" April smiled at her friend as they both remembered how their friendship began.

The girls excitedly made the rest of their plans to attend the Fireworks ride in June, although Gracie remained a little subdued, wondering how much longer she would be able to be a part of this group if she didn't have a suitable horse. She knew she could always come and spend time with them, of course, but the fact they all had the same goals, and all loved training for endurance was what kept them together.

Gracie couldn't imagine giving up endurance riding now. When she was riding on the trails, bound to this amazing creature beneath her, it was like magic.

Together they were free to explore places she would never go alone. They were accomplishing things as a team. She remembered the feeling of riding through the orchards at night on Andy when she was younger. It was like she had been touching a different part of the universe, a part she couldn't reach without a horse as her ally. Gracie had found her passion. She could do this forever. She remembered how Gallant had floated along next to her on their trail rides in the hills behind the ranch. His trot was so smooth, and he had been so eager to go down the trail, always wanting to see what was coming next. Gracie wished she'd had the chance to do this sport with Gallant. She knew he would have loved it.

Jane could see Gracie's dilemma. She appreciated all the help and guidance Gracie offered as part of her junior team, and she thought she may have found a way that could help with her problem *and* get her to the next step of her endurance career. When Harriet came to pick Gracie up that afternoon, she asked if they would both come with her for a minute. Harriet and Gracie looked at each other, neither knowing what this was about, then followed Jane to a paddock where a chestnut horse was trotting around, excited to see the three of them heading in his direction. He was a solid color, other than a small star on his forehead, and a good size at a little over fifteen hands. His trot was powerful and balanced and he moved with confidence, holding his head high, looking at the visitors as they approached.

"His name is Joshua," Jane said. "He was abandoned by his owners. They stopped paying his board and just disappeared. My contract says that after sixty days in this situation the ownership automatically switches to me so that I can sell the horse and recoup my costs. It's been three months and I haven't seen or heard from the owner at all."

"How awful!" Gracie exclaimed. "Who would do that? Just leave their horse behind?"

"Unfortunately, when you run a stable you do see this. It's rare, but it happens. Anyway, I have a proposal to make to the two of you. Joshua is a purebred Arabian. He's eight years old and well trained. A big mover but very safe and manageable. I think he would make the perfect endurance horse for Gracie."

Gracie looked shocked. She had no idea Jane had been thinking of selling her a horse. She glanced at her mother to see her reaction, but Harriet was shaking her head.

"I'm sorry, Jane. I don't think Roy will agree to buying another horse. I can ask, but I just don't see it happening".

Jane smiled. "Ahh, but I have a plan! I'm not going to *sell* Joshua to you, I'm going to *trade* him! Here's my idea. I'm always looking for safe lesson horses for my beginner riders and honestly, they can be hard to find. I propose that I give you Joshua in return for you giving me Rick and Jazz. They would fit into my program well here, and you know they would be well taken care of. Plus, Gracie, you'd be able to see them every weekend! What do you think?"

Gracie looked at her mother hopefully.

"It really might work, Mother. Daddy would have one less horse to feed and it wouldn't cost him any money for the new one. Then I would have a horse that I could really compete on, even in the fifty-mile races."

Harriet thought she probably could convince Roy to agree, for all the reasons Gracie had stated. "I think it makes a lot of sense, and I can't thank you enough for thinking of this, Jane. Let me discuss this with Roy tonight," she said. "Can we get back to you tomorrow with an answer?"

Jane agreed, and with one last look at Joshua, the three of them turned to leave. Joshua neighed at them, not happy that his admirers were leaving so soon, and Gracie laughed.

"Don't worry, Joshua," she called to the horse. "I have a feeling you'll be seeing a lot of me in the future!"

That evening, Gracie and Harriet sat down with Roy and explained how Jane had offered to trade Rick and Jazz for a younger horse more suitable for endurance riding for Gracie. Roy had a hard time coming up with any good reason to oppose the plan, and so the deal was made. Gracie found herself the proud owner of a new horse that had the potential to carry her through many years of the sport, and she was thrilled. If she started conditioning Joshua immediately, she could probably ride him at the upcoming Fireworks ride in Santa Cruz. Joshua was at a great age to begin his endurance career. His body was mature, his bones and soft tissue had been strengthened by the work he had done in the few years he had been under saddle, and he was not an overly emotional horse, which meant he would not be a danger to his rider by spooking or being difficult to manage at the start of the races where some horses became hard to control. With him, Gracie could increase her mileage and begin to plan her ride season.

Roy was quite happy with the arrangement as he felt he had unloaded a feed bill for two horses and replaced it with a feed bill for one, but it didn't take him long to realize that Joshua was a voracious eater, and an endurance horse in training for fifty-mile rides also needed grain and supplements to replenish his energy stores and maintain muscle. His feed bill cost more than Rick and Jazz combined! Roy had succumbed to Gracie's passion by now, accepting that, just like her mother, she was destined to have her life intertwined with that of a horse.

Both Roy and Harriet were surprised that Gracie had never once asked about Gallant. Since the arrival of Rick and Jazz at the ranch almost three years ago Gracie had thrown herself into taking care of the two new horses and never spoke of Gallant again. The only indication that she still had thoughts about him was that she refused to use a red halter on any other horse. Once, when she and her mother had gone to the feed store in Soquel for some supplies, Harriet had caught her daughter standing in front of the halters, staring at a red one just like the one they had given her for Gallant all those birthdays ago. The pain on her daughter's face was evident. Harriet saw the wound of missing Gallant was still raw—well-hidden, but just beneath the surface. As soon as Gracie had seen her mother watching her, she pulled herself together, put a smile on her face, and continued through the store as if nothing had happened. When Harriet tried to talk about it on the way home, Gracie had shut down.

"What's done is done" was all she would say, adding softly, "I just hope he is having a good life."

Sometimes, when she lay in bed at night, Gracie felt that she and Gallant were still connected somehow, like she could feel him waiting out there for her. She wondered if he'd found someone else to love him. Someone who could show him everything that Gracie was discovering and had a passion for. She desperately hoped that he'd found a way to be complete without her, even though she knew she could never be complete without him.

Harriet had, in fact, received a phone call from Jenny at the end of July almost three years ago. Jenny had offered to buy Gallant herself. Apparently, her young nephew had taken a liking to the horse and had been building a bond with him all summer. They had agreed on a fair price and the deal had been made. Since Gracie had never pressed her parents for details on what had happened to Gallant after he'd been sold, they had never shared the outcome of his time at the training stables with her. Neither Gallant nor Gracie knew they were each following similar paths, and that soon those paths would cross again.

Chapter Fifteen

WE RIDE IN EVERYTHING
EXCEPT FIRES!

J ack and Gallant continued to ride with Jenny and Flash, although after a while it became apparent that the bad blood between the horses was distracting them both from their training. After Flash tried to kick Gallant as he passed him one day, Jenny decided that Flash could not be trusted and stopped taking them out together. She would have to recommend to Flash's owner that he wear a red ribbon in his tail during competition to warn other riders that he could be dangerous to their horses. Flash showed so much potential and would soon be returning to his owner who would continue entering him in endurance rides. Jenny worried about Flash's future, though. His owner could be very aggressive with how he rode his horses, often pushing them too hard, beyond what they should be doing for their age and level of conditioning. Most endurance riders had a strong bond with their horses, putting the horses' safety first before getting caught up in the competitiveness of a ride. Flash's owner was all about proving what his horses could accomplish, willing to risk breaking them down too fast in order to remain at the top of the sport.

Once Flash returned to his owner, Jenny would sometimes ride Marinera out on the trails with Jack and Gallant. Marinera moved differently than the other horses he had seen. She looked so beautiful moving down the trail that Gallant was often mesmerized to the point of tripping!

"Why do your legs move differently than mine and the other horses here?" he asked her one day after they returned from a ride.

"That's because I am a Peruvian Paso! My ancestors came originally from Spain, and then from Peru. The way we move makes it easy for our riders to sit still on our backs and not have to post to a trot like your rider does," she explained.

It was after one of these rides, while Jack was hosing the sweat off Gallant's coat, that Jenny came up to the boy with some exciting news. As she listened to the way he talked to Gallant, brushing the horse till there were no signs of dirt from the trail left on his gleaming body, she knew she had done the right thing.

"Jack, I have some news for you," she began.

Jack stopped what he was doing to pay attention to his aunt, wondering what the news could be.

Jenny continued, "You know you're my favorite nephew, right?"

That made Jack laugh. "I'm your *only* nephew, Aunt Jenny" he pointed out.

"Well, regardless, you're my favorite! I've spoken to your parents, and they agree that it's time you had the responsibility of a horse of your own, so I made a deal with Gallant's owners yesterday and bought him for you, that is, if you'd like him!"

Jenny watched as her nephew's face changed from an expression of disbelief to absolute happiness. He threw the grooming brush on the ground and jumped in the air, hardly able to contain his joy.

"If I want him? I think you know the answer to that! I can't believe you bought Gallant for me! And I get to take him home?" he asked, needing her to confirm what she'd said before he could believe it was true.

Jenny smiled. She loved seeing his reaction to the news.

Jack had become so attached to Gallant that summer, and he had been dreading leaving the horse, knowing that he would be sold to someone else. Jack looked at Gallant who was tied to the hitching post, looking back at Jack like he had gone crazy.

"Sorry, Gallant," Jack said, moving closer and resting his hand on the horse's neck, reassuring him. "But this is a really big day for us. Aunt Jenny has given you to me to keep forever. Now we can plan all those rides we talked about! You'll get to come home with me to Scotts Valley and . . . wait, Aunt Jenny, where will I keep him?"

Jack said, realizing the house he and his parents lived in was not going to be an option.

"I already looked into it," Jenny reassured him. "There's a small boarding place about a fifteen-minute bike ride from your house that has room. They even need someone to help around the place and offered to offset some of Gallant's boarding fees if you'd be willing to help out on the weekends. In a few years you'll be able to drive and that will make it even easier for you."

"Wow, Aunt Jenny, you've thought of everything!" Jack said, impressed at all his aunt had done.

"Well, you are my favorite nephew," she reminded him, and they both laughed.

"You can bring Gallant back here every summer," Jenny added. "It would be good to trailer him up to Auburn and ride in the Sierra's so he can get some real mountain training at altitude. Maybe one day the two of you can even attempt to do the Tevis Cup ride!"

Jack had done some research about endurance riding over the summer and had discovered that every year since 1955 a one-hundred-mile endurance ride took place in the Sierra Nevada Mountain range. The ride started in Lake Tahoe and finished one hundred miles away in the town of Auburn. It was officially called the Western States One-Hundred Mile One-Day Ride but had become known as the Tevis Cup. Jack had secretly dreamed of taking Gallant to Tevis one day. Now that they could stay together, they were one step closer to making that goal a reality.

Once the summer was over, Jenny had taken Jack and Gallant back to Scotts Valley and helped them get settled. The next day, before she had headed home, Jack had given his aunt a huge hug.

"Thank you for everything you do for me, but for this gift especially," Jack had said.

Jenny was more like a second mother to him than an aunt and he would miss seeing her every day and riding with her. She also gave excellent advice.

"You are so welcome, Jack. I know you'll take great care of Gallant and please remember to be sensible with his training. Start him out slowly, even if he tells you he wants to go faster! He still needs more conditioning and experience before he can truly race."

"I promise I will always do what's best for him, Aunt Jenny. And if I have any questions at all, I know who to call. My favorite Aunt!"

Jenny laughed, knowing she was his only aunt also. She gave Jack one last hug, saying, "I'll see you both around Christmas!" before heading back to the stables where things would certainly be quieter without Jack and Gallant around.

*****

Jack had grown a foot taller in the last three years. His face had lost the softness of youth and he was now a handsome fifteen-year-old, with features still dominated by the kindness of his eyes. Right now, those eyes twinkled in amusement at the current antics of his horse. As Jack was brushing the dried sweat out of the gelding's coat, Gallant was trying to grab the brush out of his hand and toss it on the ground! It was a game they played often, and Jack loved that this horse, who could be such a fierce competitor on the trail, was also funny and smart, and such a pleasure to be around.

As he was grooming Gallant, Jack thought back to the first year he and Gallant had trained together. Since that first day when he had shown so much promise, Gallant had only become stronger and more confident. The bond between them had grown the more time they spent with each other.

Jack appreciated the way that Gallant had changed physically with consistent exercise and attention to diet. He had grown to his full height of fifteen-one hands. His chest had filled out, and his topline, from the base of his neck to his rump, was strong, allowing him to carry the weight of his tack and rider with ease. His rump was rounded and muscular from climbing endless hills, and the tendons and ligaments in his legs were tough and sinewy, while strong bones gave him a framework of steel to support the rest of his body. Gallant would never have the powerful presence of a horse like Flash, but he had the capacity to keep going well beyond most of his competition.

Jack and Gallant had both come a long way since their first local ride at Cooley Ranch over two years ago. Jack had convinced his father to buy an old truck and trailer so he could drop him and Gallant at the ride for the weekend and then pick him up afterwards. The base-camp was in a large field next to a creek. They parked close to the creek thinking it was not only scenic, but also a great source of water for Gallant to drink, which meant Jack had less to haul from the water tanks to his trailer. Jack thought it was strange that other rigs seemed to be avoiding that part of camp.

It had rained in torrents that night and the creek flooded its banks! Jack was awakened by Gallant nick-ering urgently as the water moved in a fast stream around his feet.

Jack had to rush to get his bag from inside the trailer, wrestle a few flakes of hay from the hay bag, which was too big to carry, and grab Gallants lead rope. The com-motion had awakened someone in the rig closest to him and a woman ran over to give him a hand.

"Come back to my rig," she yelled over the noise of the storm. "We can tie your horse next to mine and you can crash on my couch!"

Jack gratefully followed her into the dry warmth of the trailer, looking around in amazement at the inside. The rig looked like a small apartment with a bed, a couch, a dinette, a small kitchen area, and a bathroom off to one side.

The woman, Kirsten, hastily folded the couch out into a bed and threw some dry sheets and blankets on it.

"You can change in the bathroom," she said. "Then try and get a couple hours of sleep before we all have to be up for the start!"

"Will the race still go on in this kind of weather?" Jack asked, listening to the loud thundering of rain against the trailer roof.

"This is endurance, Jack!" Kirsten replied. "We ride in everything except fires!"

The next morning the rain had diminished to a drizzle. There were puddles everywhere, and in the daylight, Jack could see his trailer sitting in the middle of a small lake. He had to wade through knee-high water to retrieve Gallant's tack, which had thankfully stayed dry in the tack room. At least the old trailer didn't appear to have any leaks.

As they were tacking up their horses Jack explained to Kirsten that this was his first endurance ride.

"Then you should stay with me, Jack," she said.

"I've done a lot of rides and I'm always happy to help a young rider out and get them through their first fifty-miler. This is Pizzazz. She's a wonderful mentor for a younger horse!"

Pizzazz was a beautiful dark bay with the unusual quality of having one brown eye and one bright blue eye. Her only white markings were a star and a snip on her face. She was not a horse you would soon forget after seeing her. Kirsten had campaigned her for many years and she had done well, finally earning a decade team award for a horse and rider that spent ten years or more in competition together. Jack reassured Kirsten that Gallant was well conditioned and capable, but he would be very grateful for Kirsten's help on how to pace him in his first ride.

The ride began a little later than planned as the conditions were so sloppy and muddy that the ride manager wanted everyone to be able to see the footing they were riding through. The trail started with a short but steep uphill climb, made even harder in the wet conditions. An equally steep downhill followed, which the rain had turned into more of a ski slope. Kirsten made the call for them to dismount and lead the horses down the hill and was impressed with how Jack and Gallant worked as a team, the horse tucking his back end under him as his feet slid down the slippery slope. Gallant had never been in anything like this.

"Is this how the rest of the ride is going to be?" Gallant asked Pizzazz, who had told him she'd done this ride many times before.

"No. It will smooth out soon and we'll be able to get some good trotting in. Then we can wash the mud off our hooves at the river crossing later. You're doing great!" she added, impressed with how easily Gallant was handling the difficult footing.

"This is fun!" Gallant replied, enjoying the challenge immensely.

Pizzazz was right, the trail soon became less hilly and the horses could really move out. The rain had stopped, and the sun was shining down on them, promising an easier day with the course hopefully drying out as the race continued. Gallant could hear Jack talking to Kirsten and knew that he was figuring out what was up ahead and what speed they should be taking things.

Gallant had meant it when he told Pizzazz he was having fun. Some horses were obviously having a much harder time of it than he was, and seemed distracted and concerned with the difficult footing, but Gallant loved the challenge. He and Pizzazz were well matched as they trotted down the trail, easily navigating the shallow river crossings and taking the opportunity to take a long drink from the cool, refreshing water.

As they approached the first vet check Kirsten told Jack to hop off his horse and loosen his girth, allowing Gallant to relax and take deep breaths to lower his heart rate. The vets would not let them continue unless their horses were below the criteria of sixty-four beats per minute. Jack was confident that Gallant would pass the vet check, but when the pulse taker announced he was at fifty-two beats per minute, all those around them were impressed.

"You've done a great job conditioning Gallant for this, Jack," Kirsten observed. "After watching him for the past twenty miles I can honestly say I think you have a natural there. He just doesn't seem to get tired! The trouble is it's tempting to override a horse like that because he makes it look so easy, until it isn't anymore. It'll be interesting to see how he handles the rest of the race."

Jack was so proud of Gallant. He tolerated everything the vets did to check that he was fit to continue.

"Well, Jack, you've got yourself a good horse. Just keep doing what you're doing, and you should finish just fine!" the vet said once he was done checking Gallant.

Both horses drank their fill of water and ate some grain and hay to replenish their systems. After the mandatory hold time, the riders mounted, ready for the next section of the race.

"It's fifteen miles to the next vet check, Jack," Kirsten informed him. "We'll take this section conservatively as there are some pretty big hill climbs. It's best to know that you're saving some of the horses' energy for the final part of the ride and not using them up too early on." Then she eyed Gallant, adding, "I have a feeling it may take more than fifty miles to even get close to using this horse's energy up though!"

Gallant and Pizzazz continued on together. The trail was beautiful. Everything had been washed clean by the rains, and the leaves on the trees were glistening in the sunlight.

"What was that yucky stuff they put in our mouths before we left?" Gallant asked Pizzazz as they trotted along next to each other, their footfalls creating an even tempo.

"I call it energy-juice," Pizzazz replied. "If I don't get it my muscles cramp and I just can't seem to maintain my energy. I know it tastes weird, but trust me, you need to swallow it and not spit it out like some horses do. Our riders know what's best for us."

Gallant nodded. He realized he had a lot to learn about this sport, but so far, he felt good about everything. He could feel his lungs expanding with each deep breath, and his heart pumping strongly in his chest. He felt like his muscles were working effortlessly to carry him and Jack down the trail. Even on the steep hill climbs his back legs pushed them onwards, climbing up and up, leaving other horses who were struggling behind. Pizzazz even asked him to slow down a bit on one particularly long section, her sides heaving with the effort.

When Kirsten felt Pizzazz slowing down, she hopped off and unclipped the reins from the bit, reattaching one of them to the rope halter she had left beneath the bridle. She stepped behind her horse, the other end of the rein still in her hand and grabbed Pizzazz's tail, allowing the horse to pull her up the steep hill while she hiked behind her.

"What are you doing?" Jack asked.

"It's called tailing," Kirsten replied, her own breath deeper and more strained by the effort. "By taking the weight off my horse's back she can climb more efficiently. It's easier for her to pull me up the hill than to carry me. As you get older and heavier you'll want to teach this to Gallant."

Jack made a mental note to practice this technique on some of his conditioning rides at home, also to run the downhills more, leading Gallant behind him. He had seen some of the other riders do that and could see how it could help conserve some of the horse's energy. There was so much strategy to an endurance race, which made it even more fun in Jack's mind. He couldn't wait to learn more.

Both horses passed the next vet check easily. There were only a few horses milling around at the same time as them, and Jack was surprised to learn they were among the top twenty riders. He and Kirsten also took the chance to eat and drink at the vet check. They needed to keep their own strength up, so they could help their horses as much as possible through the last fifteen miles.

"Okay, Jack," Kirsten said. "We should mount up about two minutes before our out time, so we are ready to go. Make sure you have tightened your girth and packed yourself plenty of water and a snack. It's just as important to take care of yourself as your horse."

*****

Gallant was eager to get back on the trail. He had taken Pizzazz's advice and swallowed all the energy-juice he was given, and he felt refreshed after eating and drinking. He was beginning to figure out how important the vet checks were so that he and Jack would feel recovered and ready when it was time to get back on the trail. They left the vet check at a comfortable trot and then allowed the horses to fall into a gentle canter on some of the easier parts of the trail. They passed a couple of horse's that were ahead of them.

Pizzazz looked over at Gallant. "That feels good, doesn't it?"

"It sure does!" Gallant replied. As he had passed the other horses he'd felt a surge of excitement and a rush of adrenaline coursing through his body.

"There's a couple of easy hill climbs and descents up ahead, and then a flat section into the finish," Pizzazz explained about an hour later. "If our riders are going to race, they always pick a good section of the trail where it's safe for us to run, but I know we won't be racing today because it's your first time. You're doing so well, Gallant! Let's just keep up a steady pace and take our riders in safely, okay?" Gallant agreed. That was the most important thing of all. For all four of them to cross the finish line safe and happy from the day's effort.

*****

Kirsten was aware they only had a few miles ago and was advising Jack.

"Gallant is doing great! I'm amazed at how well he's doing for his first ride. I thought Pizzazz and I would have to really slow down and hold back to get you through, but you've matched us every step of the way!"

Jack felt his face flush at such high praise from a seasoned endurance rider.

"Listen, Jack," she continued, as they trotted side by side on a wide jeep road. "We don't need to race in and risk our horses in any way today. They have done so well for us. The most important thing is that we all cross the finish line and get our ride completions at the final vet check. Sometimes people get super competitive toward the end, and we may have some people coming up behind us and trying to race in. Just let them go. They're either experienced riders who know what they're doing, or they're taking a big risk. Either way, just let them pass, okay?"

Jack nodded. Today had been perfect and he found that right now he didn't even care what position they finished in. He understood why the saying "to finish is to win" was so appropriate in this sport. It was satisfying to know that they had conquered the trail, whether they came in first or last. Jack was proud of how well Gallant had done and extremely grateful to Kirsten for all her help.

As it was, no one raced past them in the last couple of miles and they finished the ride in sixteenth and seventeenth place, Kirsten insisting that Jack ride across the finish line ahead of her and Pizzazz. As they dismounted, they both praised their horses, each aware that it was a true team effort to be successful at any ride, and they had achieved that today, all four of them working together to make the outcome a success.

"Great job, Gallant!" Pizzazz said to the younger horse. "You did it! You are now officially an endurance horse! I'll have to keep an eye out for you if we ever really compete against each other!"

Gallant had never been more certain that he'd found the job he was supposed to do. He'd felt so alive out on the trails, challenging himself against the terrain and the other horses in the competition. Being there with Jack as part of a team, both fighting for the same goal. He glowed with pride at the praise Pizzazz had given him. Everything would have been perfect in his world if only Gracie had been there to share it with him.

Both horses passed their final vet checks with flying colors and Jack knew that Gallant had the capacity to be a great competitor if he was brought along properly. Luckily, the trailer was no longer sitting in the middle of a lake when they returned. The creek had receded, and although the ground was still rather muddy, Jack was able to put everything back in order before his father came to pick him up later that afternoon. Before he left, Jack wandered over to Kirsten's trailer to say goodbye. Kirsten gave him a big hug.

"I will ride with you anytime, Jack," she said, smiling. "I think you have a real superstar on your hands there! In a few years he will be ready for Tevis, and I will be so proud to see you there, knowing we rode your first endurance race together!"

Jack could not imagine higher praise. He and Kirsten agreed to keep in touch. Jack could not have had a better mentor for his first ride, and he would relive this adventure over and over in his mind for a long time. He couldn't wait to sign up for his next ride. Thank goodness the creek had flooded and he and Gallant had met Kirsten and Pizzazz!

*****

Three years later, Gallant had never been pulled from a race. He had completed many fifty-mile rides, first at a slower pace than he would have liked, but as he matured and became a seasoned endurance horse, Jack had allowed him to move faster along the trails, his feet barely touching the ground as he chased down the competition ahead of him. It was not uncommon for Gallant to finish in the top five in any of these races and he often found himself in first place. He made it look easy, and Gallant and Jack were making quite a name for themselves in the West Region. Jack knew that soon Gallant would have enough competition miles to attempt the most challenging ride of all, the Tevis Cup. He had three solid years of competition behind him and was eight years old. Jack now needed to line up a good schedule of rides to get Gallant's fitness level to a peak. They would have to do at least one one-hundred-mile ride before Tevis to see how they both handled the distance and to figure out their best ride strategy. First, Gallant would need a tough fifty-miler and Jack knew exactly which race he would enter him in next.

Once Gallant was put away in his stall, Jack sat down to look at the upcoming rides on his calendar.

There was an organization called AERC—The American Endurance Ride Conference. It had been formed to formalize the sport of endurance, to sanction rides, and to record the results from every race. AERC provided a calendar showing all the rides across the country, and who to contact to enter them. Since Jack lived in Scotts Valley, there was a ride very close to them called the Fireworks 50 that would take place in Santa Cruz, less than an hour from where Jack lived. The ride started at the fairgrounds and swept down a steep trail through a canyon where there was a deep river crossing. The trail then wove through the majestic redwood trees, which would allow Gallant to use his speed on the good footing as well as his technical ability on the single track that wound through the forests. Some parts of the trail even offered views of the Pacific Ocean. Jack spoke to his father who agreed to drop Jack and Gallant at the ride for the weekend, and the plan was set. Jack wondered who his toughest competition would be in the fifty-mile ride.

Gallant was feeling good. He was ready to challenge any competitor who showed up for this ride. It was, after all, his home territory. He never knew who would be there, so it was always exciting to see who was at ride camp when they pulled in. Both he and Jack were ready and anxious for the weekend of the Fireworks 50 to begin.

Chapter Sixteen

ALL WHO TRY TO CHALLENGE
ME DO SO AT THEIR OWN RISK

Flash had three years of competition behind him now. He was a fierce competitor who would hunt down the horse ahead of him, snarling as he went by, ears pinned to the side of his head. His rider always put both a red and a yellow ribbon in his tail so others would know to stay back from the large bay stallion with the intimidating mohawk. If another horse dared to get too close, Flash wouldn't hesitate to kick out, rarely making contact as he did not want to be disqualified but making his message clear: All who try to challenge or pass me do so at their own risk.

Flash had no liking and no patience for any human being. The only time Flash felt any resemblance to happiness was if he had just won a race. If he came in second or third it wasn't good enough, and if he failed to get the Best Condition Award he sulked. He had no friends. His life was about training and winning, his only goal to be the best.

He knew that this year his owner was preparing him up for the Tevis Cup, and he would finally have the chance to prove himself against the best horses in the country. He would be on a trail of historic significance that traversed mountains and crossed the American River. Parts of the ride would be in the dark, including the famous 'no hands bridge' that spanned the river one hundred and fifty feet below. It sounded like the sweetest challenge ever to Flash, who was sure he could beat anyone else that showed up, one way or another. When Flash won the Tevis Cup he would go back to his stables and take over the position of lead stallion from his father. It was a moment he would savor.

There would be a few more races along the way before he got to Tevis, the first being the Fireworks 50 ride in Santa Cruz this coming weekend. Flash was ready to get out in front at the beginning of the race and stay there. His only competition was the trail, and he must be careful not to step on a rock or trip over a tree root that could make him lame. The sheer momentum with which he moved down the trail could cause a serious injury. He didn't care if the rider got hurt, he could always be replaced, but he didn't want to risk his own chances of making it to the starting line of Tevis. He needed to stay focused, and he needed to be fast. Flash felt as if the other horses showing up to the race may as well not bother. He was there to win.

The Friday before the race in Santa Cruz, Flash arrived at the Santa Cruz Horseman's Association

Showgrounds with Dirk and Logan. Logan would be riding Flash the next day while Dirk nursed a broken toe from when Flash had "accidently" stood on it the week before. Seeing the pain on Dirk's face was well worth the beating Flash had received afterward. Flash was unloaded and secured to the side of the trailer. He was used to this routine, having done it over and over. He knew that he would be able to relax for a while and then would be taken over to the vet, who would examine him and determine if he was healthy enough to start the race the next day. They would check his body and legs, listen to his heart and his gut sounds, and have his rider lead him out and back at a trot so they could evaluate his movement, looking for any signs of lameness. His vet card would be marked with his scores, and his race number would be written on his rump with a special marker so he could be clearly identified as he went through the checkpoints the next day. Then he would be led back to the trailer, tacked up, and taken out for a short ride. Flash would always use these rides to intimidate his competitors. He would pin his ears at them, curl his upper lip, and threaten them by squealing and thrusting the back part of his body in their direction. His eyes could bore into the deepest part of a horses' soul, completely terrifying them.

Dirk and Logan led Flash to the end of the line of competitors waiting to vet in and he stood there, refusing to talk to any of the other horses and pawing the ground impatiently. These vet checks bored him, and he just wanted to get it over with.

A murmur travelled through the line of horses as a young man led a bay horse over to the vet.

"That's him," voices rippled through the crowd. "He's the one they say is the best endurance horse on the West Coast. He's been winning everything."

This got Flash's attention. If they weren't referring to him, who were they talking about? When he saw who it was, Flash felt a surge of anger.

"The upstart!" he muttered beneath his breath. The boy handling him was bigger, and the upstart had even grown bigger himself, but Flash recognized the way Gallant floated above the ground on his trot out, tail held high in the air, neck arched and ears forward. Flash could see that Gallant had learned how to put on a good show for the vets, and his confidence made him appear bigger than he was. The mares in line could not take their eyes off him. Flash felt his anger rising as he saw what Gallant had become in the past few years. He'd been wrong when he had told the whimpering young-ster that he could never be an endurance horse, but Flash sure as heck wasn't going to let him win any races against him.

*****

The vet nodded his consent that Gallant was fit to start the race and gave Jack his vet card, marked with all A's for his initial check-in score. As Jack proudly led him past the line of horses waiting to vet in, Gallant was startled by a loud, guttural scream, and looked over just in time to see a horse striking out toward him, the hoof almost making contact with Gallant's right front leg. Gallant instinctively jumped backward and looked up, astonished to find himself staring into the face of his former stable mate from Greenhill Training Stables, only this Flash was different. He was fitter, larger, and a whole lot meaner. His eyes were deep pools of hatred that bore into Gallant as he stared at him. Jack pulled Gallant away from the stallion, recognition slowly dawning on his face.

"Flash!" Jack said, then to the two men standing with him, "Get a hold of your horse! He tried to break my horse's leg!"

"Your horse shouldn't walk so close to a stallion, kid" Dirk replied, "Don't you see the yellow ribbon in his tail? In case you don't know, that means the horse is a stallion and should be given a wide berth at all times. You might want to keep that in mind."

Those around them moved a safe distance away, wondering what bad blood was between the two horses. They all knew Gallant for his incredible speed and stamina, and for the bond he had with his rider, a fifteen-year-old boy that could compete head-to-head with the adults in the sport. But none of them knew this other horse, the large bay stallion with the black eyes. His anger and hatred for the smaller horse was palpable and the group had no idea how this standoff would play out.

"What has happened to you, Flash?" Gallant asked. "I know we never got along, but you never hated me like this! What has happened to you in the last three years to make you this way?"

"You were always a dreamer," Flash sneered at him. "Always crying over your little human girl and running away from anything that scared you, yet you had the *gall* to challenge me! To tell me you could be faster and beat me at the sport I was bred for! I started to hate you at that moment." Flash's breath was coming in great snorts as he berated the other horse. "I'd hoped I was rid of you for good, but here you are, prancing around like you're special! So, here's your chance to try and beat me, you scrawny little Upstart. Tomorrow you will find out what it's like to be crushed on the trail by a real champion!"

Flash reared up, standing tall on his hind legs, squealing in fury as the crowd gasped.

Gallant stared at him calmly, waiting patiently for the display to be over and for Flash to drop down onto all four feet.

"Well," he responded then, "I sure hope you've discovered some speed since I last saw you. You'll need it tomorrow."

And with that, Gallant headed toward his trailer without a backward glance, although he could tell from the commotion behind him that Flash was spinning around, screaming obscenities across the field toward Gallant as he walked away.

*****

"You'll never guess what I just saw over by the vet check!" Penny exclaimed as she entered the area where Jane and her Juniors were setting up their camp for the weekend. Penny was known to be a bit of a drama queen, but still, the girls were intrigued.

"Well, are you going to keep us waiting to hear the exciting news?" Jane asked, and Penny, needing no further encouragement, started to describe what she had witnessed.

"There was this really cute guy with a bay horse vetting in just now, and as he led his horse past everyone waiting in line, this huge mean stallion tried to attack the cute guy's horse! He was screaming and pawing at him like they were archenemies. I've never seen anything like it. It took two men to finally control the stallion who was rearing up and screaming. I thought he was going to kill the other horse, just trample him into the dirt with his hooves. It was so scary! If any of you see that stallion tomorrow, stay away from him. I'm serious."

Penny was shaking with excitement. Nothing that interesting had ever happened at a vet check before.

"So, what did the cute guy do?" April asked. She had come out of her shell a little more over the past year or so now that she had made some friends and become more confident in her riding.

"He was as cool as a cucumber," Penny said, pretending to swoon into a chair as she spoke, making the other girls laugh. "He just told the other rider to control his horse, and then walked away, while the stallion was still going ballistic!"

Penny heaved a big sigh. "I hope he stays for the awards dinner tomorrow night. Oh! I expect he will be at the ride meeting tonight!" As the thought processed in her mind she jumped up in a panic. "I need to go and fix my hair!"

The girls laughed again. Gracie looked across to April saying, "Well, I guess we know who her crush of the week is then!"

"At least I've had a crush on something other than a horse!" said Penny as she rushed into the trailer to find her toiletry bag.

Gracie laughed, she knew Penny was just messing with her, although it was true. Despite some of the girls starting to claim they had crushes on boys at school, she'd never found one that interested her as much as her horse did.

Joshua had proven to be a fun and exciting horse to ride. He was very forward but controllable, and now that she was old enough, Gracie's parents allowed her to ride Joshua alone during the week, so long as she stuck to the trails she knew well so she wouldn't get lost. Gracie was sure that if she ever *was* lost, Joshua would easily find his way home. He always knew which direction to go for his feed bucket.

Gracie had followed Jane's advice and spent the last couple of months building up Joshua's mileage, adding either speed or distance to his training every couple of weeks, but never both together. Luckily, he already had a good fitness base when Gracie got him, so she just needed to build on that so he'd be prepared for the race. The Fireworks ride would be Gracie's first twenty-five-mile ride with Joshua, and if all went well, she would begin training him for fifties the following month. She would pace him conservatively until he had done a year or so of rides before seeing what he could do at a faster pace.

Joshua was a good horse. He was everything Gracie wanted, except he wasn't Gallant. She had given her heart to another horse eight years ago and had never taken it back. Gracie lavished extra love on Joshua, knowing he deserved it, and also to help ease her own guilty conscience. To anyone watching they made a great team. It was only in a hidden corner of Gracie's heart that she still held out a glimmer of hope that one day Gallant would return to her.

Gracie was excited to see how Joshua would do at the ride tomorrow. They had arrived early, and she had already vetted him in before the fiasco at the vet check. The girls began to get their horses settled for the night. They filled their hay bags, gave them some grain, and made sure they had plenty of water. Then they checked their tack and their vet bags, which would be sent ahead of them to each vet check the next day. Since Gracie was doing the twenty-five-mile ride with April they should finish in time to watch the fifty-milers as they came across the finish line.

Penny would be riding Jasper on a slow fifty. He was getting older but was still capable of enjoying the challenge of the ride. Jane, and her assistant Hazel, would head out to the vet checks to help the girls as they came through at various times during the day.

Gracie went to bed that night and lay awake for a while, wondering how Joshua would perform at the ride. Across camp she could hear the angry pawing and screams of a horse that she imagined may be the stallion Penny had mentioned. Soon even he quieted down, and camp became still while riders and horses alike slept fitfully, each knowing they would face their own challenges the next day.

*****

In the darkness, just before the stirrings of dawn, the fifty-mile riders made their way out of their rigs to get their horses ready for the start. Gracie had agreed to help Penny get Jasper tacked up and ready, so she rose at the same time, even though her own start time was thirty minutes later. The stallion had resumed his screaming. It sounded as if he was sending out a challenge to all who were riding that day. In the still dawn air, the sound echoed around the ride camp, adding an extra layer of tension to the anticipation of the start.

Once Jasper was tacked up and ready to go, Penny mounted and started to circle him near their trailer. She wanted to stay out of the fray of the start and go at her own pace, steady and careful, to give her horse the best opportunity of a successful day. By staying at the far end of camp away from the start, none of the girls saw the commotion as the two bay horses took their places near the starting line, their breath fogging the air as their hearts raced in anticipation of what the day would bring. Others moved out of their pathway. The rumors had flown around camp the day before that this would be a race like no other between the two horses, and all who wanted to remain safe had better stay well out of the way.

Chapter Seventeen

BE PREPARED TO EAT MY DUST

Gallant had a restless night tied to the trailer. He ate as much as he could of his dinner and drank deeply from his water bucket. He knew how important it was for him to start the race tomorrow with his body primed for the task. Jack had brought him a mash with some grain and electrolytes a couple of hours before the start of the race, then returned to his bed for a last quick hour of sleep.

Gallant didn't understand why Flash was showing him so much hatred. Last night he had screamed across camp, threatening the younger horse that he should not even attempt to challenge his right to win the race. Flash appeared to think he was the only horse capable of winning, but Gallant knew better.

There was no doubt that the stallion was in his prime. He was strong, capable, and had an intimidating intensity. His owner had pushed him hard, expecting him to win every time, at every race. He would accept nothing less. Flash had risen to the challenge by matching his own desires to that of his owner, but Flash had also seen what happened to those who failed, and that terrified him. Flash continued fighting, day after day, week after week, month after month toward the goals his master had set, losing a small piece of his soul every day in the process.

Gallant didn't know what had happened to Flash in the last few years but he showed up to the start ready to give his all, eager to see what he could do that day. He and Jack had ridden enough rides together to operate smoothly as a team. Jack knew when to give Gallant his head and allow him to cover as much ground as possible, but Gallant knew that when Jack asked him to hold back a little, there was a good reason for it. The partnership between the boy and the horse had deepened with each training mile they spent together, and every ride taught them more about trusting the other's instincts. Jack really wanted them to become a decade team, like Pizzazz and Kirsten, which meant they wouldn't try and win every race; sometimes they would compete just for the sheer enjoyment of being out on the trail together. But today was about going for the win, so long as everything went according to plan and Gallant felt good throughout the race.

Flash danced at the start, his neck arched and his tail swishing from side to side, each hoof alternately lifted off the ground as if he couldn't stand to be still. Logan looked a little terrified, realizing he was sitting on top of what felt like a volcano about to erupt. There was no denying Flash's raw power. He was impressive, and he knew it. He glared at Gallant across the space between them.

"Are you sure you're ready for this, Upstart?" Flash taunted the younger horse. "You have no idea what you're taking on by challenging me. I was just playing on those trails at the Stables three years ago. Now I know how to fight to the finish. Be prepared to eat my dust!"

Gallant didn't answer. He ignored Flash, choosing to focus on the ride ahead, to stay centered and calm, conserving his energy for the next fifty miles that would demand all his concentration and skills. He stood close to the start, focused and ready, and as the ride manager called "Trails open!" he allowed Flash to thunder past him, attacking the trail as if his life depended on it. Maybe it did.

Once Flash left in a cloud of dust, Jack gave Gallant the signal to move out. Gallant broke into a balanced trot, gliding down the trail, but hanging far enough back that he was not breathing in the dust kicked up from the other horse's hooves. Others fell in behind him. Dawn broke as the line of horses headed out, ready to take on the challenges the day would bring. A soft glow filtered through the leaves, illuminating the pathway that would start them on their fifty-mile journey.

Jack fell into the rhythm of Gallant's trot, moving his body to adjust for the terrain so his weight would stay balanced in the center and not impede his horse. Gallant was now an experienced endurance horse and knew to look ahead to plan where each hoof would fall, avoiding rocks, tree roots, and holes in the trail. He stayed focused, carrying Jack across the ground, keeping him safe as the trail snaked downwards into a canyon, the canopy of trees softening the early sunlight that rose over the distant mountains. Looking behind him Jack could see the familiar sight of horses and riders following him on the single-track trail. There was no need to race this early on, but to simply keep going, allowing the horses muscles to warm up as the riders kept an eye out for the marker ribbons guiding them toward the first vet check of the day, eighteen miles ahead.

Each ride was unique, and yet similar in many ways. Once the horses that were nervous and excited at the beginning of the ride settled into the rhythm of the trail, the riders spread out into groups that were moving at a similar pace. The sound of the horses' hooves became the music that set the tempo for the day, broken occasionally by a snort or a call to a friend ahead or behind. A nicker of reassurance passed through the ranks: we've got this; this is what we were born to do.

*****

Flash thundered down the trail. Despite what he had said to Gallant, he could feel a seed of fear in the pit of his stomach. He remembered how Gallant had moved so easily over the trails at Greenhill Stables before he'd even had any conditioning miles on him. Gallant was a different horse today. From what everyone was saying he was one of the top horses in the region, maybe even the best. Flash had arrived in camp the day before with no doubts that he would win this race, but this time he was competing against Gallant. He glanced back to see if he was coming after him already and tripped over a rock, stumbling and falling onto his knee, scraping the skin off the surface. He swore under his breath as he pulled himself up and continued onward. He couldn't afford to make mistakes like that today. He needed to stay focused, moving forward. Always moving forward. *I must rely on myself*, he thought. *I must stay strong.*

*****

Back at camp, Gracie was getting Joshua tacked up and ready. Their start would be thirty minutes after the fifty-milers headed out, and Gracie was eager to get on the trail with Joshua. She and April talked about their strategy for the day while getting their horses ready. Their goal was simply to complete the race within the designated six-hour cut off time, and finish with happy, healthy horses who would be ready and willing to take on the next challenge in another month or so.

Gracie and April would have a vet check twelve and a half miles into the ride with a forty-five-minute hold to allow their horses to eat, rest and be checked over by the vets. They had been warned at the ride meeting the night before that since the fifty-mile riders had left thirty minutes ahead of them and had an extra five and a half miles on their first loop, there was a strong possibility that the front runners would arrive at the vet check at the same time, or even ahead of some of the twenty-five-mile riders. This could make the vet check quite congested. The fifty-mile riders would do a further twenty-five-mile loop with their final vet check just seven miles from the finish, while the twenty-five-mile riders would head back toward camp on the same trail they had been on that morning.

Gracie knew that they would have to cross the river heading out and back that day. Because there had been so much rain this year, ride management had taken extra precautions at the river crossing. The riders would need to follow the safest pathway that ride management had indicated. There would be volunteers on each bank to help guide the riders to the correct entry and exit point, and they would have walkie talkies to call for help if anyone got into trouble.

The beginning of the twenty-five-mile ride was uneventful and the sun was well in the sky as Gracie and April arrived at the river crossing. The bank where they entered was muddy from the many hooves that had already gone before them in both the fifty and twenty-five-mile races. The bank was slick which made entering tricky. Both horses navigated it well, Milarky spurred on by Joshua's confident attitude, trusting his friend and following him bravely into the murky water. The volunteer pointed out that the best path to take was toward a certain tree on the far bank. As a precaution a few volunteers stood further downriver on the opposite bank in case a horse got into trouble. Gracie could feel Joshua's strong legs plowing through the moving water.

She called to April behind her, "How is Milarky doing April? Are you okay?"

Above the sound of the moving water, she could just make out April's tentative reply.

"I, I think so..."

Gracie knew that April was not comfortable with river crossings, but she had come a long way in the past year or so, and she and Milarky had bonded as a team, learning to trust each other more and more under any circumstance on the trail. Jane had reminded them often that bravery could not be found unless there was fear first. If April kept going despite her fears, then she was braver than most.

"You're doing great, April," Gracie encouraged her friend. "Just put Milarky right on Joshua's tail. We're almost there."

No sooner were the words out of her mouth than she heard April scream. As Milarky lost his footing, the strong flow of the water immediately turned him downstream. He scrambled to get his legs back under him.

"Keep going!" the volunteer yelled to Gracie, seeing she was about to go after her friend. They had been told during the ride meeting that if one horse lost its footing in the river, the other horses should continue on the correct path. It was easier for the volunteers to deal with one rider in trouble than a whole group.

It went against Gracie's nature to leave her friend, but she realized that if she kept going it might encourage Milarky to turn back toward Joshua and keep him from getting into any further trouble. She pushed Joshua on to the other side and they scrambled out, turning immediately to see what was happening to April and Milarky.

Milarky was even more panicked now that Joshua had left him. He struggled to find his footing, his body momentarily slipping under the water until he managed to secure his weight onto all four legs below him.

Gracie yelled to the volunteer on the other bank, "Can you send another horse and rider in to guide him across? He'll do better if he can follow someone!"

Gracie saw the volunteer turn to talk to the small group waiting to cross. A woman on a grey horse moved forward, nodding to the volunteer as she moved out into the water.

"April," yelled Gracie. "Look at where that rider is. Head toward her if you can, put Milarky right behind her horse's tail to follow her across!"

April knew that she had two choices. She could fall apart, wailing and screaming for help, leaving her horse to fend for itself, or she could pull herself together and keep a cool head, helping Milarky to regain his footing and get them both safely to the other side. She chose the latter. With words of encouragement from the volunteers, April managed to guide Milarky through the deeper water until he got closer and closer to the grey horse. Once he saw the other horse in front of him, his panic lessened and he fell in behind the horse and rider as they guided them to the far bank where Gracie was waiting.

"Thank you so much," April said to the woman as she exited the river wet, tired, but safe just a few feet farther downriver from Gracie and Joshua. The volunteers cheered and clapped, the riders still waiting to enter the river whooped and hollered to April saying what a great job she had done, making mental notes themselves on what to do if their own horse got in trouble.

"You were fantastic, April! You and Milarky both were!" Gracie said as she rode up to her friend, reaching across the distance between their horses to give her a big hug. Now her fear had subsided, April was grinning as she praised her horse for his bravery. She and Milarky had put their trust in each other to overcome a scary situation and they had succeeded, coming out stronger on the other side.

"Did you see Milarky?" April said excitedly. "Wasn't he amazing?"

"Yes!" Gracie responded. "And so were you. I'm so proud of you both!"

The girls began moving down the trail once more, eager to reach the first vet check so their horses could rest and eat before the second half of the ride. So far it had been a good day, maybe not in the way they had anticipated that morning, but certainly April had more confidence in herself as a rider, and more appreciation for how much her horse would give her when she needed it. Gracie wondered how the day could possibly get any better.

Chapter Eighteen

It Is a Race, after All

Flash had surged ahead at the start and had stayed ahead. This was how he liked to win races. He started fast, and he finished fast, Logan hanging on for dear life most of the way, unable to hold the stallion back even if he wanted to. Flash never gave a thought to his rider. He would have done the race by himself if he could have. He knew that all he had to do was follow the ribbons strung along the trail to the next vet check. At the vet check he always came in hot, requiring his tack to be stripped and cool water to be poured over his neck and down the insides of his legs to try and cool him down. His respiration tended to stay high, and it could take several minutes for his breathing to calm and his body temperature to cool down so he could reach pulse criteria and be allowed to continue through the vet check. Most riders would not choose this method for getting their horses through a vet check as they could lose a lot of time waiting for their pulse to drop.

Flash figured he was far enough ahead of the other riders that it wouldn't make a difference if he took some time to get his pulse down, so when he reached the first vet check he stood by the water tank taking huge gulps of water to rehydrate while Logan stripped the saddle off his back. Within a few minutes Flash heard another horse coming in, being hand walked into the vetting area by his rider. The horse's girth had already been loosened and the horse looked relaxed and calm.

It was Gallant! After tripping early in the race, Flash had stayed focused, watching the trail he was speeding along to avoid another fall. He hadn't heard the other horse behind him and assumed he had a decent lead. How had Gallant made it here so close behind him? Then he remembered how lightly Gallant traveled. Flash was now getting a taste of what his prior stable mate could do.

Jack led Gallant over to the pulse takers who placed the stethoscope along his girth line, just behind his left front leg. After thirty seconds the pulse taker called "Time!" and Gallant's time was recorded, indicating his pulse was at criteria and his hold would begin right then. Gallant would get to leave the vet check ahead of Flash who had still not pulsed down.

Flash raised his head from the water tank and pinned his ears back as Gallant approached. Jack led his horse around the far side of the tank, keeping as much distance between the two horses as he could, not trusting that Flash wouldn't try to lash out at Gallant as he had the day before.

Gallant dropped his head and took a drink, one eye on Flash the whole time.

"Just because you leave a couple of minutes ahead of me doesn't mean I won't hunt you down on the trail and get ahead of you again, Upstart!" Flash said.

"I fully expect you to try, Flash," Gallant replied calmly. "It is a race, after all. The trouble is you are too big and bulky. Your heart rate won't come down fast enough if you don't pace yourself, so I'll just keep passing you at every vet check."

Flash stomped his foot toward the young upstart and squealed at him.

"You can try as hard as you like, but I am The Almighty Flash, and I am the best horse here today! I haven't lost a race yet and I don't intend to start losing now. When you hear me coming up behind you on the trail you'd better move out of the way or I'll run right over you and your precious boy!"

Gallant took one last long gulp of water and moved away from the tank, looking back at Flash with a few final words, "Don't get yourself too worked up Flash, you haven't even pulsed down yet. You should try and relax!"

As Flash squealed again, throwing his head up in the air, Gallant calmly walked over to be vetted through.

Gallant had done this many times now and knew to stand quietly while the vet made sure that he was doing well and not being overly stressed by the competition. The ride vets took their jobs very seriously and would not send a horse back out onto the trail if they felt the horse was compromised in any way, indicating they could have a problem between there and the next vet check.

The vet nodded to Jack, indicating that he wanted to see Gallant move, so he trotted him out toward an orange cone placed about a hundred feet away from where they were standing. At the cone, Jack turned Gallant around and trotted him back toward the vet. The vet took Gallant's heart rate one more time, then looked at Jack and nodded.

"He's looking great! You have a fine horse there, young man, with great impulsion and a good attitude. Good luck with the rest of the race!"

Jack thanked the vet and led Gallant away to find his crew bag among all the others that had been brought out to the vet check earlier. Jack knew they had a long twenty-five-mile loop ahead next, and both he and Gallant would need to refuel and hydrate well for that long section of trail.

Gallant watched as Flash was vetted through. He stood still for the vet, ears pinned back the whole time. When it was time to trot out, Flash dragged Logan out to the cone and back, yanking on his arm and shoulder, almost knocking his rider over. Jack shook his head sadly. There was obviously no love lost between those two. As many miles as they must have done together they had formed no bond or relationship that would make the sport a pleasure for both, regardless of where they placed at the finish. In the right hands Flash could have been an amazing horse, but whatever had happened to him over the years had made him mean and surly, and Jack suspected that even if he had a different owner in the future, it was too late to undo all the damage that had been done to the Stallion's mind.

Jack looked at Gallant, eating his alfalfa and his bucket of mash, relaxed and happy. If Gallant had shown any signs of stress at all during the ride, Jack would have slowed him down, even getting off his back and walking for a while if necessary, whatever it took to help the horse finish. There was no race worth winning that would make him endanger his horse in any way. Jack knew the same could not be said for Flash. That horse would be pushed to win at every race until he was finally pushed too hard. What would his future be then?

*****

Gracie and April dismounted once they were about half a mile from the vet check. They loosened their horse's girths and clipped their reins onto the halter so they wouldn't yank on their sensitive mouths as they led them in. April was still gushing about her dramatic river crossing, while Gracie was reflecting on the first half of the ride with Joshua. He really was an amazing horse. He had done everything she had asked of him on the trail, moving out with confidence and listening for her cues. She knew she would have had a very different race experience if she'd been riding Rick in this race. She was having to hold Joshua back so that Milarky wasn't being pushed too hard, and Milarky was the more experienced horse!

"I wonder what's happening in the fifty-mile race with that mean stallion and the other horse," Gracie mused as they walked into the vet check. "I suppose we might see some of the top fifty-milers if they haven't gone out again already."

"I don't want to see them," April replied. "I don't like the sound of that stallion and I don't want him anywhere near Milarky!"

Gracie looked thoughtful. "Maybe Penny was exaggerating. You know how she can be sometimes. If he were that bad, he would get disqualified, or someone would file a protest against him or something. Remember that a protest can be filed if any horse or rider acts badly at a ride or does something against the rules."

April agreed. Maybe Penny *had* been exaggerating the day before and the stallion wasn't as scary as she'd made him seem.

When they arrived at the vet check it was bustling with activity. It seemed that a lot of fifty-mile and twenty-five-mile riders had come in close to the same time, and the volunteers were running around trying to make sure that all the horses and riders had everything they might need. There was hay for the horses, enormous bags of carrots that the ride manager had provided, and plenty of fresh water for them to drink. There were also smaller buckets of water with sponges in them that the riders could use to cool down their horses who were sweating from the exertion of the trail. The vets were working hard to vet all the horses through in an orderly fashion, while crews waited for their riders to come in, having laid out everything they would need from the crew bags.

"I don't see Jane or Hazel anywhere," April said, looking around.

"They may not have made it here yet," Gracie pointed out as they joined a couple of other horses at the water tank. "Let's find a spot off to the side where we can set our stuff up, and then you can hold the horses while I go and grab our bags," Gracie suggested.

Despite the number of horses at the vet check, they managed to find a spot with a little shade to keep the warm sun off the horse's backs. They gave the horses some hay so they would be happy to stand together with April while Gracie went in search of the bags.

As she was looking, Jane and Hazel appeared. Jane was looking slightly flustered.

"I'm sorry! We didn't see you come in," she said, a little out of breath from running over from the far side of the vet check area. "We were watching the first-place horse in the fifty head out. It was that young man Penny was talking about. He only has about a three-minute lead over the stallion so it's all very exciting. The stallion's over there going ballistic again, and the rider's trying to find someone to hold him so he can get back on! I was so happy to see you'd come in so I'd have an excuse to say no if he asked me. You saved the day!"

Gracie laughed, and then looked toward the commotion. She could just make out the large bay stallion, the rider clinging on desperately as the horse danced around, lifting his front feet in half rears and tossing his head as he got angrier and angrier that he wasn't allowed to leave down the trail yet. Luckily, a few seconds later the out timer yelled, "Go! You can leave!" and everyone around breathed a sigh of relief as the horse took off at a gallop.

"Wow," said Gracie. "I sure am glad I'm not riding that one! As magnificent as that stallion looked in all his frustrated glory there's not a sane rider on earth who'd want that beneath them!"

Gracie had never been so grateful to return to Joshua, who looked up from the hay he was eating to nicker gently, welcoming her back. Jane and Hazel helped them sort through the crew bags to find dry socks for April and mash for the horses. The girls both refilled their water bottles and ate a snack.

"Did you see that stallion?" Gracie asked April as she put together the mash buckets.

April nodded. "I'm really glad he left!" she said. "Imagine being the poor horse he's chasing down!"

"With only three minutes between the top two horses there's no doubt that the stallion's going to catch whoever's in front of him, especially at the speed he took off," Jane pointed out.

"Let's get through this vet check and get back to camp before the fifties finish," Gracie said. "This is one finish I absolutely do not want to miss!"

Chapter Nineteen

TRYING TO MAKE THE MOST
OUT OF A DIFFICULT SITUATION

J ack and Gallant had taken off down the trail at an easy
   canter. They would go at a decent pace over all the
good footing, slow down over rocks or areas that could
be dangerous at speed and try to keep moving forward
at a pace fast enough to hold the lead. Jack knew he had
about three minutes before Flash would be leaving the
vet check and he intended to make the most of that time.

Gallant floated over the ground in his usual style,
leaning into the bends of the trail, fluid and strong,
never tripping or breaking his pace. Jack gloried at the
gift he had been given with this horse. They had become
more and more attuned to each other with each race
they completed and every training mile they shared.
Jack already knew that Gallant was special. Even though
he hadn't done endurance on any other horse before
him, he had watched the other horses on the trail and
he could see that as amazing as many of them were,
Gallant had something *more*. It was an intangible thing,

hard to explain, and Jack also liked to think that it wasn't only Gallant by himself that was special, he hoped that it was the two of them together that made their partnership magical. Jack felt in his bones that Gallant could make history one day, and he fully intended to give him that chance.

Gallant was happy with this new life. He had found the adventure's he had been looking for. He still thought of Gracie often, and wondered where she was and what she was doing, especially when the nights were quiet and he could see the moon high up in the night sky, bathing him with its glow. Last night, when he was tied to the trailer and the moon was shining down on the ride camp, he almost felt as if she were there, where he could reach out and touch her. Gallant knew that part of his life was over, that he was with Jack now, and he was grateful that he had been given such an amazing second chance, but he would never forget Gracie.

Gallant shook his head, bringing himself back to the present. He had to focus on going down the trail so he wouldn't trip, or if he did, he needed to be alert so he could regain his footing quickly, keeping Jack centered above him where he wouldn't get hurt.

Just a few minutes out of the vet check, Gallant heard the thunder of hooves behind him. Flash! He had known he would be coming after him, and he had expected it, but there was still something ominous about hearing his approaching hoofbeats and his heavy breathing.

"Let me by, Upstart!" Flash snarled.

Even if he wanted to, there was nowhere for Gallant to move off the trail safely. They were on a single-track with barely enough space for one horse, let alone for another to pass. On the left was a steep uphill with trees scattered across the hillside, the forest floor was covered in leaves that had fallen over the years, wet and slippery after the recent rains. On the right was a downhill slope, dropping about fifty feet to a small creek that wound itself along a canyon floor in gentle curves and undulations, making its way to the river they would cross again later.

Flash continued to breathe on Gallant's rump, trying to push the younger horse along, forcing him to pick up his pace to stay ahead of the stallion. Gallant heard Jack yell something to Flash's rider, but it didn't change anything. They all knew that Flash was controlling his own ride, the human was merely perched on top, hoping he would survive the experience.

Gallant felt as though he was being physically pushed from behind by the force of Flash's energy. He had to focus on not losing his footing, especially as they reached a downhill section of the trail. He knew that if Jack could have found a place to pull over and let Flash pass, he would have, but they were locked in by the topography around them. There was nowhere to go but forward. Gallant could hear Jack cursing under his breath.

Suddenly, Gallant saw Flash jump to the left onto the high bank of the hillside and try to blow past him.

He was now alongside Gallant but several feet higher, his feet scrambling on the slippery leaves as he tried to keep moving forward to pass the other horse. As Flash slipped and lost his footing he plowed back down onto the trail, landing heavily beside Gallant and shoving him onto the downhill slope to the right. There was nothing Gallant could do except try to keep his feet under him as he went off the edge. He felt Jack give him plenty of slack in his reins, allowing him to use his head and neck to find his balance. Jack stayed centered, staying out of the way as his horse tried to recover his footing and slow down, avoiding trees and branches that could have knocked his rider off his back. Gallant scrambled, controlling his downward trajectory but feeling his legs slip out from under him over and over again. Jack didn't panic. He knew his partner would figure out what he needed to do, and before long Gallant managed to pull up to a halt about twenty feet below the trail.

He looked up to see Flash hammering along at breakneck speed without even glancing back to make sure that he and Jack hadn't been hurt. It was a credit to Gallant's natural athleticism that the situation had not ended up with both of them in a tangled heap by the creek below, injured, or worse.

No other riders were around to witness what Flash had done or they could have reported the incident and had Flash disqualified from the race. Slowly, still a little shaken, Gallant pulled himself back up to the trail and picked up an easy trot. He felt Jack reach down and rub his neck.

"That was a close one, Gallant. You did good, boy. You kept us both safe."

About an hour and a half later, Jack and Gallant entered the final vet check out on the course. They had done forty-three of the race miles so far, with only seven miles to go. Gallant felt good. He knew he had all the energy he needed to finish the race strong. No other horses had passed them on the trail, not only because of their speed, but because the other riders knew it was best to stay well out of the way as the two front runners faced whatever private battle they were fighting out on the course.

Flash stood there panting by the water trough, his heart rate hovering well above criteria so he couldn't pulse down and start his hold time. Gallant again walked in on a loose rein, completely relaxed, and just like last time, he pulsed down within a minute of entering the vet check area. While Gallant took a long drink from the water tank, Jack and Logan exchanged heated words about the incident earlier.

"I have never seen such bad sportsmanship from a rider," Jack said, noticing as he spoke that Logan was pale and appeared rather shaken.

"I'm sorry, really. This horse is impossible to control. He's fast but he doesn't listen to anything I tell him. When I pull on the reins, he just takes the bit in his mouth and does exactly what he wants, which is usually run faster."

Jack's own temper calmed when he saw how sorry Logan truly was, but regardless, he had allowed Flash to knock them both off the trail.

"I don't know what to tell you. Maybe you should consider just stopping here if you don't think you can control him," Jack suggested.

"I can't do that! You have no idea what it's like working for this guy! I can't afford to lose my job." Logan replied. "I'll do my best, but one way or another I have to get back on this beast and finish the race. I'm sorry again."

Gallant figured the man probably had no control over what Flash was doing, and this meant that he would have to be extra careful that Flash didn't do something stupid on the last seven miles of the course that could cause harm to him or, worse yet, to Jack. He had never forgotten the horror of seeing Gracie lying on the ground, hurt and bleeding, and he never wanted to see that happen to someone he cared about again.

Gallant looked over at Flash and saw the desperation in the horse's eyes. It was obvious the stallion was tired. Gallant could tell he was probably pushing himself harder than he ever had, trying to stay ahead of the lighter horse. Logan was pouring water over his neck and the insides of his legs, anywhere he could to try and cool the large horse off and bring his heart rate down. Flash stood with his head low, breathing hard and trying to recover. Gallant addressed him, letting his anger about the earlier incident dissipate.

"Flash, we only have seven miles to go. Let's just take this at an easier pace for a while. There's no one even close to us back on the course so we don't need to push this hard! What if we go easy until we reach the river, then we can race in and may the best horse win. Whatever happens, we'll be taking first and second place and our humans will be proud of our efforts. More importantly, we will be safe and sound to race another day."

Flash looked over at Gallant for a moment, deep in thought. Why would the other horse offer him what could be a chance to recover and win? Because he was weak, Flash surmised. Weak from years of being an emotional puppet at the hands of the humans. This was Flash's chance to take back control of the race.

"So," he countered. "You'll give me a chance to catch up and pass you after you leave the vet check, and then I can set the pace until we reach the river? I'm warning you though Gallant, after that I fully intend to fight you for first place. For me, anything other than first may as well be last."

Gallant agreed. He knew this was not exactly a truce between them, but it was the best he could do, even knowing that Flash would now have a chance to recover by going at a slower pace and could very well beat him in the last few miles. He also knew this was a much safer way to approach the rest of the race against such an unpredictable opponent. He was trying to make the most out of a difficult situation.

Chapter Twenty

THERE WAS NO NEED FOR
FORGIVENESS BETWEEN THEM

G racie and April had finished their ride, returning to camp happy and elated with their horses' performance. April had gained more confidence in her horse, and in her own abilities to get through the tough sections of a ride. The girls had finished in the middle of the pack of twenty-five-mile riders with sound horses that passed their final vet check easily. Gracie fixed herself and April some sandwiches and chips, hungry after their long ride. After checking the horses one more time to make sure they were eating and drinking well, they grabbed a couple of camp chairs and headed toward the finish line to sit and wait for the fifty-mile finishers to start coming in. They were eager to see if the stallion and the other horse had maintained the lead, and if so, who would cross the finish line first!

When Gallant left the vet check for the last seven miles of the race he settled into a slow trot, occasionally even slowing to a walk if he came across some particularly technical trail. For the first few minutes Jack allowed him to pick his pace, wondering if the horse had some minor discomfort from being pushed off the trail earlier that could have stiffened up during the hold at the vet check. After a few minutes though, Jack asked him to go a little faster, not feeling any changes in Gallant's gait that suggested any discomfort, and unaware of the agreement Gallant and Flash had made at the water tank. For the first time ever Gallant purposefully ignored his rider's commands, holding the trot but also holding back and not going at his usually animated pace.

Jack waited another few minutes then asked him to pick up the pace again. He knew that Flash would soon be coming up behind them and he didn't want a repeat of the incident earlier. Again, Gallant held his trot, as if he were on an afternoon stroll at home, not in the last few miles of an endurance race he was currently winning! Jack was confused. He had carefully checked Gallant's tack to make sure there was nothing that could be irritating for him over the last seven miles, and he had lifted and checked each hoof to make sure there were no small rocks that had become wedged between his frog and hoof wall that could make him lame. Everything had looked good. Jack had no idea why Gallant was not acting like himself.

They had gone a couple of miles from the vet check and were riding on a slight downhill along a jeep trail with good footing. In a few miles they would meet up with the river once again. This was a place where they should be making up time at an easy canter.

Jack saw Gallant's ear flick back, hearing a sound in the distance behind them. Jack turned, knowing what he would see but hoping it wasn't true. Flash was gaining on them at an easy trot, his big, powerful stride pounding along the road, getting closer with every second. Jack squeezed with his calves, encouraging Gallant to move out, and once again Gallant ignored him.

Flash cruised by on their right, overtaking Gallant and giving him a quick nod of the head as he passed, acknowledging the other horse. Amazingly, Gallant fell in behind Flash, picking up his pace to match the easy stride of the horse in front and they moved down the trail in unison. Flash's ears were forward, as were Gallant's, neither horse pressing nor crowding the other. They maintained a steady, effortless pace, picking away at the miles as they headed downhill toward the river crossing. Jack was astounded, as was Logan who turned back to Jack with his mouth hanging open. This was a completely different meeting than the one the horses had earlier. It was almost as if the two horses had reached a truce. Both riders relaxed their reins and let the horses pick the pace, moving down the trail together, focused, but breathing easily, neither appearing to be stressed by the other's proximity.

As they made their final turn toward the river, with only a little over a mile to go after the crossing, their energy changed. Both horses became more tense and focused. The race was back on! Flash plowed into the water ahead of Gallant, his powerful legs cutting through the surface, his neck stretched ahead, straining to keep moving forward, his large body sideways to the current that moved the water downstream.

Gallant knew this was where he had to gain back his lead. He scooped some of the water into his mouth, taking a few deep gulps, hydrating himself for the big push to the finish, which he knew was mostly uphill once the river crossing was completed. Then he surged forward, his huge lungs keeping him higher out of the water, as opposed to Flash's dense weight that pulled him downwards. Flash, seeing Gallant pulling forward on his left, tried to slam his larger body into the other horse, hoping he could force him to lose his footing and be pulled downstream, but Gallant was ready. Just as Flash moved sideways, he leaped forward, cutting in front of the stallion and clearing a pathway to lunge for the far bank ahead of his opponent.

Flash found that he was pushing against thin air! He struggled with his balance, his body turning downstream, being dragged to the left by the strong current. His legs were swept out from beneath him. For a few moments he struggled frantically, churning through the fast-moving water, searching for anything solid to stand on. He could feel his back sinking lower, and he desperately lifted his head as high as he could, gasping for the air that may disappear at any moment. Logan was panicking, envisioning the horse being swept away by the powerful current. He was pulling on his reins in every direction, trying to get his bearings and turn the horse's head toward the far bank. Just as he was about to bail and try to swim for the shore, he heard a voice above the water's roar.

"Loosen your reins," Jack shouted from the shore, he and Gallant having paused to make sure the other horse was not in a life-threatening situation. They could have continued onwards, taking advantage of what was happening to Flash to make a solid lead for the win, but neither horse nor boy were so deep into the competition that they would allow another being to suffer without trying to help, even Flash.

"Give him his head so he can balance and turn, he knows where he needs to go," Jack yelled again.

The volunteers were watching anxiously as the scene played out, one of them on a walkie talkie to ride management to let them know what was happening. When Logan heard Jack above the noise of the water and the panic in his brain, he released the reins, allowing Flash to move with the current toward the other bank, until his feet finally touched firm ground again. Once in the shallower water Flash was able to walk against the current toward a break in the bushes where he could exit. Everyone breathed a sigh of relief. Flash stood there taking deep heaving breaths, not even having the energy to shake the water off his soaked body.

Gallant, seeing the stallion was out of danger, turned toward the trail and took off at a gallop. Jack gathered up his reins, knowing exactly what Gallant was planning to do. They had come down this part of the trail that morning, and both knew that after a long flat fire service road, the trail would take a sharp right onto a series of steep switchbacks that would carry them up and out of the river canyon, eventually emerging to the edge of camp where the finish line would be set up. Gallant was sure that Flash would not come after him. It had taken all of Flash's energy to turn himself around and swim out of the river toward the shore. It was doubtful that he would be able to gallop uphill for a mile to the finish. Gallant slowed to a steady canter, covering the ground easily, sucking in deep regular breaths, his body working just as it had been trained to do, prepared for this very moment.

As the girls sat waiting for the first finishers, rumors began to fly about the two lead horses. It sounded like there had been some trouble at the river crossing with one horse finding himself in danger. It had apparently been touch and go for a few nervous minutes until he had managed to pull himself to the shallower water.

Flash stood at the riverbank, water dripping off his back into the mud beneath his feet. His lungs burned with the effort of finding his way out of the sweeping current. He was exhausted. He had never pushed his body this hard before. He didn't have to. The thought of losing the race took hold in his brain. He remembered all the horses at his barn that disappeared overnight. He shuddered. Flash gathered his thoughts, shook himself, and surged forward, ready to take chase. He couldn't risk losing. Not today. Not ever.

Gallant kept moving, now cantering steadily up the hill. Turning at each switchback and continuing up, up, knowing he would soon be at the finish. At one switchback Gallant glanced back. Flash was coming after him! How he had found the willpower to overcome his physical exhaustion Gallant would never know. He had to admire the tenacity of the stallion. He was a worthy, albeit dangerous, adversary. Gallant moved faster, knowing that he had to keep ahead of his opponent. He couldn't risk Flash getting too close to him. Who knew what he would do in those last few moments to try and win?

As Gallant turned the final corner, the finish line just a couple of hundred feet ahead of him, he glanced back for one final check. Flash lunged around the corner right behind him, breathing heavily, a crazed look in his eyes. Logan was pale faced and hanging on to the front of the saddle having lost all control.

There were a lot of people hovering around anxiously, wondering which horse was going to be in the lead. When they saw the boy with the bay horse burst out of the final switchback the crowd began to cheer, the cheer turning to a collective gasp as the stallion that had challenged him exploded from the trail, just seconds behind.

Gallant had flown across the finish line with a burst of speed that few other horses had, especially after having raced fifty miles. As Jack brought him to a halt, a roar erupted from all those watching. Gallant stopped, turning to watch Flash cross the finish, defeat already registering in his eyes. He wanted to go to Flash and tell him how well he had done, how hard he had worked and how proud he should be, but as the cheering of the crowd died down Gallant heard only one thing. The sound of Gracie's voice crying out his name!

*****

Gracie had been on the edge of her seat as the finish unfolded, April squealing with excitement next to her. They were jumping up and down cheering for both horses, their athleticism and courage obvious to all who were watching, when Gracie suddenly stopped. She put her hands up to her mouth, her eyes not believing what she was seeing. It took a moment for her mouth to form the word, and for her feet to obey the command from her brain to move, but then she was running, running toward the horse she had not seen in three years, yelling his name over and over! He was bigger, more muscular, but she would have recognized him anywhere. He was here! Gallant was here!

Gallant's head turned toward her, his eyes lighting up in recognition. Jack had jumped off and was standing by his side stroking his neck, but Gallant ignored him. As he saw Gracie running toward him Gallant felt his legs moving, not sure how he was being drawn toward her, but knowing that he needed to be. He closed the distance between them, still not sure this was real.

As Gallant came to a halt in front of her, he dropped his head into her open arms and closed his eyes, breathing in the sight and smell of the person he had loved since the moment he was born. She was really here! Her soft hands and sweet voice were indeed saying his name over and over. She wasn't hurt anymore! She was fine, and she loved him! There was no need for forgiveness between them. Everything was as it always had been—a girl and the horse she loved.

Gracie burst into tears from sheer joy and did what she had done so many times before, and what she had been wanting to do since the day of the accident. She buried her face in his mane, breathed in his smell, her hands roaming across his face and neck as if she couldn't get enough of him. And in that very moment, two broken hearts became whole once again.

PART THREE

Chapter Twenty-One

I Can't Ever Give Him Up

Jack had no idea who the girl was that had her arms wrapped around his horse's neck as she cried into his mane. He and Gallant had just fought for a courageous win at the Fireworks 50 against Flash and Jack would like to be celebrating with his horse himself, but Gallant had melted into the arms of this stranger instead.

Flash's owner, Dirk, came stomping over to the horse that had fought valiantly, albeit aggressively, coming in a close second. He was shaking his fist at Logan, yelling at him that he hadn't pushed Flash hard enough and had cost him the win. Logan, white-faced after being carried up the final hill at breakneck speed, was now red-faced and angry.

"That horse is a danger to his rider and to everyone around him," he yelled at Dirk. "You've created a monster! I should never have gone along with the inhumanity you call a breeding program. Kingdom Stables should be wiped off the face of the earth and you should never be allowed to go near another horse again. I swear I will put a stop to you, I will expose you and your sham of a stables, even if it's the last thing I do!" With that, Logan dropped the reins and stormed off, shaking his head in disgust.

Flash was standing with his head hanging low, knowing he had been defeated. Dirk grabbed the horse's reins, jerking his head up and dragging him away from the finish line muttering, "What a useless beast. I guess I'll have to ride you myself from now on to show you how it's supposed to be done."

Jack couldn't stop himself. He took one look at Gallant, still mooning over the girl crying into his mane, and tossed her Gallants reins. "Watch him for a moment," he commanded as he marched over to Dirk who was dragging the once proud stallion away.

"You ruined that horse!" Jack shouted, within ear-shot of everyone at the finish line. He normally wouldn't speak to an adult like that, but he was disgusted by the attitude of the owner.

"I knew Flash up at my Aunt Jenny's training stables. He was always proud, but you have made him mean! You have driven him to believe he must win at any cost. One day, because of you, he will really hurt someone, or hurt another horse, and it will be your fault."

"No, boy," Dirk sneered back at Jack. "One day, this horse will win the Tevis Cup because he has trained hard and been pushed to excel. I won't tolerate a horse in my barn who doesn't give one hundred percent at every race, and Flash will pay for falling short today."

Jack could not believe what he was hearing. "Fall short?" he exclaimed, his arms raised by his sides, questioning the sanity of the man before him. "Fall short? That horse gave more than everything he had. He almost drowned fifteen minutes ago! He had to use all his energy to haul himself out of a fast-moving river, and yet he still chased my horse up twenty switchbacks at a gallop to try and win this race. He deserves to be recognized for his efforts, not condemned for them!"

Dirk shook his head and continued to drag Flash back toward his trailer. Jack knew that Dirk wouldn't bother to show Flash for Best Condition, an award given to one of the top ten horses to cross the finish line who the vets deemed physically superior that day. Dirk saw his horse's accomplishment as a failure and would treat the horse as such. Jack shook his head sadly as he watched them leave.

Speaking of Best Condition, Jack needed to get Gallant ready to show. He only had one hour after they crossed the finish line to present Gallant to the vets for his judging, and Jack knew that Gallant would show well. He was tired but not exhausted. He had given a tremendous effort, but he had not been run into the ground, and after a bucket of mash and a cool tub of water to replenish his thirst, he would be as good as new. Jack would groom him until his coat was gleaming and present him to the vet looking as fresh as he had at the beginning of the day.

He walked over to Gallant who looked at him as he approached. The girl spoke as soon as he reached to take Gallant's reins from her.

"Hello, I'm Gracie," she began. "I'm so sorry for acting that way, but I haven't seen Gallant in three years, and I didn't know if I would ever see him again. We grew up together at my family ranch in the Valley of Heart's Delight. My parents sent him to a training stable and then sold him. It wasn't their fault. We were told he wasn't safe to be ridden."

Tears sprung up into Gracie's eyes again, threatening to overflow. "Oh my gosh, to see him bursting through that trail out of the canyon and galloping across the finish, I just couldn't believe it was him!"

Jack looked at the girl, realizing she must have been the previous owner. "Gallant was in training with my Aunt Jenny, and she bought him for me. I am the only person that has ever ridden him," Jack explained. "I need to get him ready to be shown for Best Condition now, but maybe we can talk later."

He started to lead Gallant away, but the horse wouldn't move, refusing to leave Gracie's side. Jack felt betrayed. If Gallant was making a choice between the two of them, then Jack was the one left empty-handed. He did the only thing he could do at that moment. "I don't suppose you'd like to come to my trailer and help me get him ready?"

Gracie nodded, a huge smile breaking out on her face, and with Gracie and Jack walking side by side toward the trailer, Gallant was more than happy to follow.

"Oh, wait a moment!" Gracie said, stopping suddenly, realizing she was walking away from her friend with no explanation. She turned toward April, who had been watching all this drama unfold from the sidelines, as had most of the people in camp. "April! I am so sorry. I got so excited to see Gallant again, I didn't mean to ignore you."

"Are you kidding me?" April replied. "That was the most beautiful thing I have ever seen. Go and be with Gallant, I will check on Joshua and the other horses and catch up with you later."

Gracie thanked April and continued walking, feeling as if she were in a dream. She could not believe she was reunited with her horse after all this time. As the reality settled into her mind, she also realized she had a major problem. As wonderful as it was to see Gallant, he wasn't hers anymore. It was obvious that this boy, Jack, had built a relationship with him and would not be ready to hand Gallant back to her, even if she *could* persuade her parents to buy him back. Plus, she had Joshua now. He had proved today that he had the potential to be a wonderful endurance horse. But how was Gracie supposed to walk away from Gallant now that she had found him again? He was her everything. She knew now that she would never love another horse like she loved him.

Jack could see the girl was deep in thought, and he had a feeling that he knew where her thoughts were going. By now they had arrived at the trailer and Gallant sunk his nose deep into a bucket of mash. Jack checked he had enough hay so that as soon as he had finished his mash, he could continue replenishing all that his body had depleted over the fifty miles of trail. Jack silently handed Gracie a brush, and they started brushing the dried sweat off Gallant's coat as he ate, one on each side of him.

Gracie, now that she had a few minutes to settle her thoughts after the dramatic reunion, suddenly found herself a little shy and tongue-tied, having just realized that Jack was probably a few years older than her and extremely good looking. She had admired how he stood up to the owner of the horse that came in second, and how he hadn't really freaked out when a complete stranger had run over to his horse and thrown herself at him, bawling into his mane.

Gracie looked at the coat she was brushing and felt Gallant's body beneath her hands. He had grown. This wasn't the skinny, gangly colt she had spent so many hours of her childhood with. This was a fully grown, mature horse, who had been well taken care of, and who had become an elite athlete under the care of this boy opposite her.

"Gallant looks wonderful, Jack. He's really matured since I last saw him. You've obviously given him the best care."

Jack looked over at the girl. He could tell she was probably trying to figure out where this situation was going to end up for her and Gallant. But Jack was not giving Gallant up, ever. The sooner Gracie knew that the better.

"Thank you," Jack answered, brushing the tangles out of Gallant's mane.

"I was the only one he would trust to ride him when we met. It was like he had a horrible experience and just shut down. I don't know why he picked me as the person he could trust, but we connected like I have never connected with another horse before, and he has become my best friend. My partner. I can't ever give him up."

Gracie's eyes threatened tears again, but she nodded her understanding. "I was the first human to ever touch him. I snuck into the birthing stall seconds after he was born and lay down with him, soothing him. His mother, Magri, let me touch him all over. I could feel his heartbeat against my own. We were hardly apart after that for the next five years. On my tenth birthday I had this crazy idea to ride him," Gracie cringed at the memory, ashamed of her ignorance. "I just assumed he would let me climb on his back and that would be that. Well, he didn't know what was happening and he spooked, dumping me on the ground. I was pretty badly injured, I even blacked out for a few minutes. When I came to, my father told me they found me on the ground with Gallant hovering over me, completely distressed. I can only imagine how scary it was for him." She stroked his neck lovingly, grateful to have been given a chance to finally reassure him after that awful day, to show him she was fine and how much she still loved him.

"I was taken to the hospital and when I came home the next day Gallant was gone. He had been sent to your aunts for training. I was lost without him, but I thought he would be home in a few months, and by then my leg would be better. I had hoped I would be able to show him that I was okay, but your aunt told my parents that he couldn't be ridden, that he wasn't safe, and so my parents agreed to sell him. My heart broke the day they told me he was gone forever. I didn't think I would ever see him again. Jack, I am so grateful that I got this chance to know that he is fine. More than fine. It means more to me than you will ever know."

Gracie offered Jack a tentative smile. She didn't know how this was going to go, but she knew that at the very least she had the opportunity to keep track of Gallant now, and maybe even see him again. It was not the same as having him home, but it was something.

Jack swore silently to himself. He had hoped to show for Best Condition, grab some sleep, and head home, never having to deal with this girl again. Why did she have to be so nice? And why did he get the feeling that Gallant would not want to be separated from her any more than she wanted to be separated from him a second time. This was really going to complicate things. Hearing her story, he knew how hard it must be to know that Gallant belonged to him now, and yet she was reassuring him that she understood the situation and was grateful to be given the chance to see her beloved horse again. They obviously had quite the history together. Now that Jack could see the bond between them, he was more than a little worried about how he would separate Gallant from Gracie. As close as Gallant and Jack were, there was something different about Gallant's demeanor when he was around this girl.

Jack shook the thoughts from his head. Right now, he needed to focus on getting Gallant ready to show for Best Condition. They could figure everything else out later.

Chapter Twenty-Two

YOU'RE LIVING IN MY STALL

Jack and Gracie led a gleaming and refreshed Gallant over to the vet check area to show him for the Best Condition award. By then, several other riders had crossed the finish line and the top ten for the day had been established. Other riders would still be coming in over the next several hours, some barely making the twelve-hour cutoff time, but they would be thrilled they had completed their goal of finishing the ride that day.

The head vet, Dr. Sears, motioned for Jack to bring Gallant over. Gracie followed just behind them. The vet scribe had Jack's vet card, showing how Gallant had done at the vet checks throughout the day, and they would now judge him on how he looked an hour after he had finished the race. The judging was done on a points system, based on the time the horse finished, the weight of the rider and tack, the scores from his final vet check and his vet scores throughout the day.

Jack held Gallant still while the vets examined him. They listened to his heart rate, his gut sounds, checked his muscle tone and checked him for tack galls. Once the hands-on check was done, the vet asked Jack to trot Gallant out in a straight line for about a hundred yards and back, just like at the other vet checks. Then he was asked to trot in a large, complete circle in each direction so the vets could further check for lameness, impulsion, and the horse's overall attitude.

Once Jack and Gallant returned, the vet took Gallant's heart rate and once again made a notation of the beats per minute on his card. Once the judging was complete, the vet shook Jack's hand and told him that Gallant looked great. Gracie was beaming with pride at seeing how admirably Gallant managed himself at the Best Condition judging. Jack had trained him well. He was responsive, his ears were forward, and his trot showed that he had plenty of energy left after the long ride. He was certainly "fit to continue," which was what the vets were looking for.

Now it was a waiting game while the vets looked at any other horses that had crossed the finish line in the top ten and decided to show. The results would be announced that evening at the awards dinner in front of the other riders.

"Well," Jack said, looking at Gracie. "Thanks for all the help getting him ready. I think he has a good shot of winning BC. He looked fantastic, even after such a tough race."

Jack glanced around and saw that Flash's owner had already pulled out of camp without giving his horse time to rest and recover from the day. Jack shook his head sadly.

"Flash was in the stall next to Gallant at my aunt's training stables," he explained. "We even rode together a few times. He was very competitive back then and was very jealous of Gallant, but I never imagined he could become so mean. Now that I've met his owner, I can see how that could have happened. It's so sad to see what could have been such a great horse abused like that."

Gracie couldn't imagine ever treating a horse that way. She felt sorry for the stallion, realizing he could have been quite different if he had been raised with love like Gallant had been. Why was life so unfair, giving some the best start in life, while others had to suffer and fight for every scrap of opportunity they could find? Gracie was happy that Gallant had been surrounded by love from the moment he was born, and that even now, without her, he was still well loved and cared for.

Gracie realized there was a lot she didn't know about Gallant's life since he had left the Valley of Heart's delight, and she really wanted more time with him, and with Jack, to fill in those gaps.

"I don't suppose you and Gallant would like to come over and hang out by our trailer for a while, would you? I need to wait for my friend Penny to come in off the fifty, and I need to check my horse. It was his first twenty-five-mile ride today." Seeing Jack's hesitation, she added, "I know you don't know me, and all this is very strange, but I would love to hear more about Gallant's life since

GALLANT

you've had him, and I could tell you all about his first five years. He used to get up to some really funny antics!" Gracie looked at Jack hopefully. She wasn't sure how she could walk away from Gallant right now, and she needed to see if she and Jack could come to some kind of agreement where she could see Gallant again.

Jack didn't really want to hang out with a bunch of thirteen-year-old girls, but he wasn't sure he could get Gallant away from Gracie anyway. "Sure," he agreed. "Let me go and change and get cleaned up a bit, and then we'll be right over." As he tried to lead Gallant back toward his trailer the horse once again stopped. This was becoming more than irritating.

"Look," Gracie suggested. "Why don't you go and freshen up and I'll take Gallant to my trailer. I have plenty of hay and water there for him." At Jack's obvious reluctance she added, "I promise I won't steal him or anything! He will be at my trailer when you're ready to come over."

Jack gave her a sheepish grin. The thought had indeed crossed his mind that Gallant could have been whisked away by this girl, back to wherever he had been raised, but he also realized that was a crazy thought. Gracie knew that his Aunt Jenny knew her parents, and besides, he had a feeling he could trust this girl.

"Okay," he acquiesced. "I'll see you in half an hour," and he continued back to his trailer to get changed. Gallant nickered to him, but then willingly turned and followed Gracie as she led him in the opposite direction. Jack wondered why he had this sinking feeling that he and Gallant's connection may be in jeopardy. If he took the horse home and didn't allow Gracie to visit him, Gallant would be sad. When Gallant saw Gracie at an endurance ride, he would be distracted and unable to focus. On the other hand, if he allowed Gracie to become part of Gallant's life again, would the horse go back to loving the girl so much that it left no room in his heart for Jack?

Gracie could not believe she had Gallant all to herself for the next half an hour. Before returning to the trailer where she would have to face everyone's questions, she walked Gallant around the edge of camp, stopping at a large water tank to allow him to drink. The last time she had led him around like that had been at the ranch in the Valley of Heart's Delight. Gracie reached out and touched Gallant's forehead, then gently stroked the irregular white marking that ran down his face and spread out across his muzzle. She knew his markings like they were a part of her own body. She had drawn his face so many times on her homework that even her teachers would probably recognize this horse. Just the fact that she could reach out and touch him now, like she had so often in her dreams the last few years, was an absolute miracle to her. Gallant nuzzled into her shoulder, asking her for more attention, and Gracie laughed. He had changed, yes, but in some ways, he hadn't changed at all.

Gallant was with Gracie again. After all the craziness of the day, the most perfect thing had happened. He had found Gracie, or she had found him. She was taller, but she still sounded and smelled the same. Her laugh was exactly as he remembered, like music and magic rolled into one. When Jack had tried to lead him away from her, he just couldn't move. He didn't want to upset Jack, but he was afraid that if he let Gracie out of his sight, he may never see her again. When Jack and Gracie took Gallant back to the trailer together Gallant was in heaven. This was how he wanted it to be. He wanted them both with him, all the time. He knew he had to make the most of every second with Gracie in case he had to go back home to the stables without her. Was there any way for him to explain to them that he loved each of them? That he wanted to be with both of them if he could?

Gracie led him to get a drink of water and sat talking with him, just like she used to. Before long, she stood up and walked him over to a trailer where she introduced him to two other horses who were tied there. Gracie put some hay on the ground for him to eat and then sat in one of the chairs next to another girl, still holding Gallant's lead rope as if she, too, couldn't bear to sever the connection between them.

April was at the trailer and was desperate to know how things had gone with Jack after they had left.

"Gallant was amazing showing for Best Condition," Gracie told her friend. "He looked great and I'm sure he has a really good chance of winning." Gracie looked back at Gallant with her eyes shining. "I can't believe it was him at the finish. I never imagined that would happen."

*****

Gallant saw Jack approach. After checking Gallant over he joined the girls, taking one of the empty seats opposite them. Both girls seemed to get a little quieter, and the mood changed as soon as Jack joined them.

That was interesting, Gallant thought. While the humans talked, Gallant turned to the chestnut horse closest to him—Joshua, he thought his name was—and asked him if he had raced that day.

"I did my first ride with Gracie," Joshua explained. "She says we did really well, and we're going to train for a longer ride next time. I can't wait to get back to my paddock, though, and just relax at home. The moon will be beautiful over the pear orchards this evening."

Gallant's ears pricked up. "Do you happen to live at a ranch in the Valley of Heart's Delight?" he asked the chestnut, already suspecting he knew the answer.

"Yes, I do!" Joshua replied. "Do you know it? I live in the first stall nearest the ranch house, with the big paddock that runs alongside the driveway."

Gallant felt the first stirrings of jealousy, but before he gave into it, he desperately needed to know the answer to a question, so he asked Joshua as pleasantly as he could, "Is there a mare there, a grey mare, who goes by the name of Magri? She might have a foal by her side?"

Joshua nodded, not realizing the impact of his words on the bay horse next to him. "Yes!" he nodded enthusiastically. "She's wonderful! She was the first friend I made when I moved there. She's in the paddock right next to mine. How do you know her? Have you visited our ranch before?"

Gallant turned toward Joshua slowly.

"You could say that" he agreed. "Magri is my mother, and you're living in my stall."

Chapter Twenty-Three

HOW WAS SHE SUPPOSED TO SAY GOODBYE

P enny was surprised to find her two best friends sitting at the trailer talking to none other than the cute boy she had spotted at the vet check the day before. "Well thanks a bunch," she snorted as she approached the group, Jasper trailing behind her. "Don't worry about us at all. It's not like it's been a long day or anything."

"Oh, my goodness! Penny! I'm so sorry," Gracie said, jumping up. "What can I do to help? Oh, this is Jack by the way, and this is Gallant!"

Penny's eyes grew large as understanding dawned on her.

"*YOUR* Gallant?" she asked, not noticing Jack flinch at her words. As Gracie nodded her head in excitement, Penny added, "But how? Where? Oh my gosh, I missed so much!" Gracie and April laughed.

"Let's get Jasper settled and then we can fill you in," Gracie offered.

Gracie handed Gallant's lead rope to Jack while she helped Penny get Jasper untacked and brushed off. Gracie made sure he had plenty of hay and water while Penny made him up a mash. This left the very shy April sitting with Jack trying to think of something to say to keep the conversation going.

Jack decided to help her out and asked, "So where do you all live? And where do you keep your horses?" He was really trying to figure out how far away Gracie lived so he could be prepared when she asked if she could see Gallant again.

"Oh, well," April stammered, "I live on a ranch near Morgan Hill and Penny lives in San Jose. Gracie lives in the Valley of Heart's Delight. She keeps Joshua at home at her ranch and her mother trailers him over on the weekends so she can ride with us. Where do you and Gallant live?"

"We live near Scotts Valley," Jack replied, realizing they all lived in close proximity to each other. The thought did not make him particularly happy. "Gallant lives at a boarding place about a fifteen-minute bike ride from my house so I see him almost every day and I do my training rides from there."

By now, the other girls were back from caring for the horses and Jack looked over to Penny. "How was your ride?" he asked.

"Pretty good, actually. How was yours?" Jack, Gracie, and April looked at each other for a moment and then burst out laughing.

"It was interesting, thanks!" Jack finally answered.

Gracie added, "Gallant won! He looked amazing coming across the finish! Well, so did Jack. I mean, he won too, obviously, not that he looked good coming across the finish. But he did. Oh shoot." And for the first time in Gracie's life she sat there blushing at a boy.

Penny was not happy at the beginning of the growing friendship that she had missed out on, so she proceeded to monopolize the conversation until Gracie could see that Jack was getting uncomfortable and was ready to leave.

Gracie intervened. "Well, it must be getting close to the awards dinner. Jack, shall we take Gallant back to your trailer and then go and get our places. I'm so excited to see him get Best Condition!"

"It's not a done deal yet, Gracie," Jack admonished gently, not wanting to jinx his chances, although he felt reasonably confident that Gallant did well. But he agreed to her suggestion and they both rose to walk Gallant back to his own trailer.

"We'll see you over at the awards dinner in ten minutes," Gracie told the other girls. "Save us a seat if you get there first!" and she and Jack left.

"Well," said April, looking at Penny. "I know Gracie is thrilled to see Gallant again, but it doesn't hurt that he's owned by a cute boy who seems really nice!"

"Hmmm," Penny replied, crossly. "Gracie is just trying to figure out how to get her horse back. She's only being nice to Jack so she can see Gallant again. Besides, she's two years younger than him. He wouldn't be interested in a girl who's only thirteen."

"You're just saying that because you have a crush on him and you're fourteen already!" April said, laughing. Penny had not been very subtle with her interest in Jack, but April was not sure it had been reciprocated. Jack had just been too polite to get up and leave sooner.

The girls checked the horses one more time and headed over to the awards dinner to get a table for everyone. They wondered where Jane and Hazel were. They had been coming back from the vet check and should have been back to camp at least an hour ago. In talking to Jack, the girls had lost track of time and only now realized that something must have happened to detain them. They hoped it wasn't something bad.

*****

Dirk pulled into Greenhill Training Stables late that evening. It had been a three-hour drive from Santa Cruz, and he had driven as fast as he could, the trailer swinging around the turns behind him. Jenny met him in the driveway. Dirk had arranged for Flash to stay at Greenhill once again as it was centrally located for all the rides on Flash's schedule that summer. Since Jenny had worked with Flash before, Dirk had hired her to keep Flash conditioned in between his endurance rides.

Jenny was appalled when she saw Flash being led out of the trailer. The horse was clearly exhausted. His tack had been removed back at camp so he could be seen by the vets and get his completion, but then Dirk had thrown him in the trailer without adequate feed and water and had not even run a grooming brush over him. Since Albert was off the clock for the night, Jenny took Flash and bathed him herself, putting him into a stall afterwards with a mash and plenty of hay and water. She would have words with Dirk in the morning.

Flash recognized where he was, even though it had been three years since he had been at Greenhill Stables. Last time he was here he had been training for his first competition. This is where he had met Gallant, a young, scrawny upstart with no confidence who was constantly whining about being homesick. Flash was never home-sick. His home was not a place he had fond memories of. It had all the luxuries of a high-end training facility, but there were unspeakable things that went on there.

Flash was one of the lucky ones that had made it to adulthood. Even then, many of his friends disappeared as they were sold, or sent to the kill-pen auctions when their performances were too mediocre to be consid-ered worth feeding them anymore. Those that remained knew they had better perform or a similar fate would await them.

Coming in second that day at the Fireworks ride was not only a personal humiliation for Flash, it might also cost him his life. If he didn't do better next time, he might find himself being trucked to Mexico to become dog meat rather than trucked to the starting line at Tevis.

Flash knew he could not make any more errors. He must win the next race at Virginia City at all costs. Whatever he had to do, he must win.

*****

The awards dinner had gone well, and as predicted Gallant had won Best Condition in the fifty-mile race. The girls cheered as Jack went up to collect his prize, a beautiful horse blanket with the name of the ride on it and large embroidered letters that said "Winner – Best Condition."

Toward the end of the dinner the manager made an announcement specifically for Jane's Juniors, saying that Jane and Hazel had experienced a flat tire coming back from the vet check and it had taken a while to get it fixed. They wanted to let the girls know they should be back soon and not to worry. The girls breathed a sigh of relief that nothing worse had detained them. Then they realized how much they would have to catch up on when they got back to camp!

After dinner was done and everyone helped clear tables and stack the chairs, Jack and Gracie walked back to check on Gallant, who was relaxed and munching away on his hay. He looked great. Gracie gave Gallant a hug and congratulated him on winning Best Condition.

"I think this is all still sinking in," she said, looking at Jack. "I still can't believe I am here, with Gallant. And that he has become this amazing endurance horse! If he couldn't be with me, then I'm glad he ended up with you, Jack."

Jack smiled. Gracie really was a very cool girl. She was sincere and honest. She said what she was thinking but considered the other person's feelings while she was doing it. He could see why Gallant had loved growing up with her. He knew what she was going to say next, though, and he dreaded that his reply would upset her.

"So, obviously I would love to stay in touch and see Gallant again. I heard you tell April that you live in Scotts

Valley which is only thirty-minutes from my ranch. Maybe you could come and ride with me sometime? Gallant would love to see his old home again."

Jack looked at Gracie's hopeful face and inwardly cringed as he spoke. "The thing is Gracie, it would be hard for me to get Gallant over there. I work part time at the boarding stables to offset Gallant's costs and to pay for my ride entries. Between that and training I just don't have much time. Plus, Gallant and I will be going up to my Aunt Jenny's in a couple of weeks once school is out for the summer. We'll be going to endurance rides from there, and I'll be working at her training stables. I'm not saying you won't see Gallant again, of course you will, but I just don't know how to make it happen on a regular basis. I'm sorry."

Gracie had been building up her hopes all afternoon thinking that she and Jack would find a way to make this work. She was sure her mother would take her over to see Gallant if Jack would allow it, but it looked like they weren't even going to be in Scotts Valley after the next couple of weeks, and there was no way that Gracie could get to Auburn where Jenny's training stables were. How was she supposed to say goodbye to Gallant again so soon?

Gracie took a few steps back, struggling with her emotions. "I understand," she told Jack. "Thank you for taking such good care of him. I just don't know how to say goodbye to him again, so I have to go!"

With one last agonizing look at Gallant, Gracie turned on her heels and ran back toward her trailer, tears falling down her face as she left. She could hear Gallant calling for her, but she knew she couldn't go back. She had to find a way to be happy knowing he was doing well and that she would probably see him again at other rides in the future. It was better than nothing, but Gracie couldn't fix the empty feeling she had from finding her best friend and losing him again so quickly.

When she got back to her trailer her friends were there, as were Jane and Hazel who had been filled in on what happened that day. When Gracie arrived crying, they all rallied around to offer comfort. She appreciated their efforts but knew they would never understand what she was truly going through. How many times would her young heart be broken?

Chapter Twenty-Four

I Can Offer You a Great Life

In the morning, Gracie arose first and went outside to check on the horses. She wasn't sure whether to go and find Jack and try and say a proper goodbye to them both. She was embarrassed at how she had run away from them last night and wasn't convinced she wouldn't embarrass herself again if she gave it another shot. But the decision was made for her when she saw that Jack had already left ride camp. He must have left early, and Gracie was upset he hadn't told her he was leaving or given her a chance to say goodbye to Gallant, even though she had been the one to run off the night before.

So here she was again, with the same hole in her heart as always. It helped knowing that Gallant was fine. He had found a job he loved, and a person who loved him, but Gracie still felt that she and Gallant were meant to be together. There was no way that she could go through her life knowing he was out there somewhere and not be able to see him. She just needed to figure out a way to make it happen.

*****

Jack was embarrassed at how he had arranged for his father to come and pick them up so early that morning, sneaking out of camp before Gracie had the chance to change her mind and come to say goodbye. He hadn't wanted to see how Gallant was around Gracie again. Before yesterday he thought that he and Gallant had the most special relationship a human and a horse could have, but now he felt like the runner up in a contest. When Gallant was with Gracie, he was different. He was *home*. Jack recognized the ugly feeling of jealousy. He didn't want to feel this way, but he didn't know how to stop it. When they had driven out of ride camp Gallant had called and called for Gracie, not stopping until they were several miles down the road. Would he ever forgive Jack for taking him away from her?

When Jack called his aunt later that evening to tell her how the ride had gone, he was too embarrassed about his own behavior to mention that Gallant had met up with his original owner again. He told Jenny about the way they had battled it out with Flash though, and all the other horse had done, both good and bad, to fight for the win. Jack told her how disgusted he had been with Dirk and his reaction to Flash coming in second.

"It was truly awful, Aunt Jenny," Jack told her. "I just don't understand how anyone can treat a horse that way. Flash tried so hard. Even though he was awful to us on the trail I could still recognize what an amazing performance he put in, especially at the end when he raced us up the switchbacks to the finish."

Jack sensed the hesitation in Jenny's voice before she responded to him.

"Jack, I need to tell you something. Flash is here. Dirk brought him up here last night. He had arranged for Flash to spend the summer here as we are close to where his next races will be, and Dirk had asked me to keep him conditioned in between. Dirk headed back to Arizona this morning. I'm giving Flash a week off and then I'll start working with him again. If I had known all this, I might have decided differently, but it's too late now."

Jack was stunned. He could hardly believe that Flash was up at Greenhill Stables right now. In a way, he was happy that the horse was away from Dirk, but he was worried for his aunt's safety after watching Flash's performance on the trail at Fireworks.

"Aunt Jenny, please don't get on him until I get there next week, at least not out on the trails. Flash is a different horse from who he was three years ago. He's meaner, and even more driven. He almost broke Gallant's leg when he first saw him! Please promise me that you'll be really careful until I get there."

Jenny was touched by her nephew's concern, but she felt she knew Flash well enough and could handle the horse. She was more troubled about his owner. The more she got to know Dirk the more she realized she didn't want him as a client. She didn't like how he treated his horses and it sounded as if he had only worsened over the last few years. She would have to think about how to handle him in the future.

Jenny and Jack said their goodbyes and Jack hung up the phone feeling extremely nervous about Flash being at his aunt's stables. He needed to get there sooner and decided he would talk to his parents that evening about heading up earlier than planned. He also realized that it offered him the chance to get Gallant farther away from Gracie just in case she decided to try and find them.

*****

Gracie went home with Joshua and hesitated to tell her parents all that had happened over the weekend. They were the ones who had sold Gallant and now here he was, doing endurance with Jack when he could have been doing it with her. Gracie had never felt resentment toward her parents before, but now she questioned their decision all those years ago. Had they known that Gallant was being ridden when they sold him? Why had Jenny said he wasn't safe when her nephew had apparently been riding him just fine? Could her parents not see how miserable she had been all those years away from Gallant, and if they had, how could they not have gone searching for him sooner to bring him home? It didn't add up. Gracie felt like the whole world had ganged up on her and Gallant to keep them apart. Worst of all was the feeling that her parents, the two people she loved most in the world, had betrayed them.

Gracie walked over to the barn to check on Joshua and visit Magri. She and Magri had become close after Gallant had left and Magri had taken Gallant's place as the keeper of her secrets. The grey mare whinnied as she approached and stood quietly while Gracie entered her stall.

"Oh, Magri," Gracie sighed. "I have some news for you and it's mostly good, I guess, but sort of bad also. I saw Gallant this weekend."

Magri nuzzled Gracie's neck as if she understood, encouraging her to go on.

"He looked amazing, Magri. He was tall and strong! He won the whole race and came away with the Best Condition award. I was so proud of him! The thing is, he has a new owner now, and I don't think he wants to let me see Gallant again." Gracie thought back to how nice Jack had been, but underneath she could sense his concern about Gallant having a relationship with her again, where Gallant would always be torn between the two of them.

"I feel like I've lost him all over again, Magri. It's so bittersweet to know that he's okay but that I can't see him. How can they all have turned against me like that, knowing Gallant and I should have been together?" Gracie felt the pain in her heart slowly turn to anger against those who had been a part of their separation.

"I'm going to find a way to see him again, Magri. Last time he left I was a child and had no choice, but now I'm older and I have a will of my own. I know what I want, and I'll find a way to get it. No one will stop me!" Gracie cried into Magri's mane, but this time they were not the cries of a little girl who had lost something precious. This time they were the cries of a young woman who felt angry, betrayed, and determined to take charge of her own destiny. She just had to figure out how to make it happen.

*****

Gallant was devastated. He had gone from the exhilaration of winning the race, to the sheer joy of seeing Gracie again. He had spent wonderful hours with her, almost like old times. But he had also discovered that Gracie had Joshua now, the horse that had taken over his stall next to his mother at the ranch. Gallant desperately wanted to see his mother again and let her know he was okay. He supposed that Gracie would try and tell her, but he didn't know how much his mother would understand. When Gallant thought of Joshua living in his stall he shook with jealousy. Joshua was living the life that should have been his, and although he was grateful for everything that he and Jack had accomplished, he still felt like his real destiny had been stolen from him.

When Jack came to check on Gallant later that day, he found a horse he hardly recognized. Usually Gallant was friendly and curious, always up for whatever Jack had planned, but today Jack found a horse sulking in the corner of his stall who wouldn't even walk over and greet him.

"Gallant," he said, holding out his hand and inviting the horse over. "I know this is difficult for you. It's difficult for me as well, but what am I supposed to do? I can't give you up! We've been through so much together. I don't know what I would do without you." Jack hated to even say her name, not wanting to remind Gallant of the girl. "I know you miss her. I can understand why now that I've met her and heard your story, but I think you will learn to love me just as much, and I can offer you a great life and endurance career. Don't give up on me now, okay?" Jack pleaded.

Gallant did not move. He was too caught up in his own pain to feel badly about Jack's. He pawed the ground angrily, staring at Jack and wondering how this person he trusted could have ripped him away from Gracie once again. It was just like last time. He may not have been whipped, but he may as well have been. The pain was just as great. Gallant knew he and Gracie were meant to be together. Why was the universe making that so difficult?

MAYBE THERE COULD HAVE
BEEN A BETTER WAY

G racie sat with her parents and siblings at the dinner table. She was pushing the food around her plate, only taking the occasional small bite and clearly distracted. Harriet couldn't stand it any longer.

"What on earth is wrong, Gracie? You've been moping around ever since you got back from the Fireworks ride a couple of days ago. I thought you said Joshua did well?"

"He did great," Gracie agreed. "I think I'm just feeling a little out of sorts now the race is over and school finishes tomorrow. I feel like I want to do something new and exciting, but I also want to earn some money toward Joshua's keep and my ride entries. I think I'm just feeling a little lost, that's all."

Harriet looked across the dinner table at her husband. They had talked about offering to send Gracie and Joshua to a riding camp for a few weeks over the summer. Jane had told her of a few camps up toward the foothills where the girls could bring their own horses and try other fun riding disciplines with them, like show jumping, or obstacle courses. Maybe offering her the chance to do that would bring Gracie out of her current moodiness. When Roy brought it up, however, they didn't get the excited response they expected.

"That's so sweet of you, and normally I would love to do that, but I had another idea that I wanted to run by you," Gracie replied.

Gracie had been lying in bed last night when the idea came to her. She knew exactly where Gallant would be this summer because Jack had told her they were going to his Aunt Jenny's as soon as school was over. All Gracie had to do was get herself to Greenhill Training Stables and she could be with Gallant again.

"I was wondering if you could give the trainer, Jenny, a call. I thought that maybe she could use some help over the summer, and I'm sure she would let me take Joshua so I can keep him conditioned. I'm strong for my age and I know horses. I'm sure there are all kinds of things I could do to help. Clean tack, sweep out the barn, muck out stalls, whatever she needed. The summer must be a busy time for her with all the horses coming in for training. I could be like a student helper. I could work in exchange for room and board and a small allowance to help me save for my expenses with Joshua, and in return she would get a really hard worker. Plus, she's one of the top trainers in the country and I could learn so much just by being around her."

Gracie thought of one more thing that might persuade her father. "I'm sure that camp you were thinking of costs quite a lot of money, Daddy, and this wouldn't cost you anything."

Roy and Harriet were surprised at Gracie's suggestion, but it did seem to make sense, if Jenny was looking for someone.

"Doesn't Jenny have a nephew that helps her out in the summer?" Harriet asked Roy. "I seem to remember her mentioning him a few years ago."

Gracie almost choked on her food. So, they *did* know about Jack and hadn't said a thing to her! They must have known that Jenny was buying Gallant for Jack. Gracie had felt bad for not telling her parents the whole reason why she so desperately wanted to work at Jenny's stables, but now she felt no remorse at all.

"If she does, I'm sure he's there to help her ride the horses, not do all the menial things that I would be doing," she said carefully. She knew if she acted too anxious to go her parents would get suspicious. She needed to stay calm and focused on the conversation.

"Well," Roy spoke up. "I suppose there's no harm in asking. Your mother can call Jenny after dinner and see what she says."

Gracie smiled to herself. Step one of her plan was going well. If Jenny said no, she wasn't sure what she would do next, but she would find a way to get to Auburn and to Greenhill Stables one way or another. Knowing

Gallant would be there waiting for her would make everything worth it.

*****

Harriet hung up the phone and asked Roy if she could talk to him in his study for a few minutes. "I just got off the phone with Jenny. Apparently, she often takes students over the summer to help her at the stables and learn more about riding from her at the same time. If they're not local, she gives them their own room and feeds them. They get an allowance each week and they help with feeding, grooming, and chores around the stables. Jenny's nephew, Jack, has gone there every summer for years and that's how he met Gallant. Anyway, Jenny is more than happy to have Gracie as one of her students this summer. She could take Joshua with her, and Jenny would be responsible for them both. What do you think? I know this would be a dream come true for Gracie, but she's still quite young to be gone for so long."

Roy thought about it for a moment before answering, "I think she would be in good hands with Jenny. And yes, she's only thirteen but she is quite mature for her age. I think this would be good for her."

"Should we tell her then, Roy? She's going to be so happy!" Harriet was glad that things were going well for her daughter. She knew after the accident and losing Gallant that Gracie had a difficult time coping. It was wonderful to see her thriving and happy, enjoying endurance riding with her new horse. Everything had worked out even better than Harriet had hoped.

Everything had worked out even better than Gracie had hoped. When Harriet called Gracie into the study and told her the news, Gracie smiled, realizing she now had the opportunity to spend the whole summer with Gallant. She could hardly believe she would get to see Gallant again in only a few days!

Now that part of her plan was in motion, Gracie had to consider what Jack's reaction would be when he saw her there, and how Jenny would feel when she found out that Gracie had orchestrated this whole thing to be close to Gallant. Jenny may send her right back home for being sneaky and underhanded. Gracie had never acted this way before, but she also hadn't known how everyone had worked so hard to keep her and Gallant apart. Her parents, Jenny, and Jack had all played a hand in keeping her away from the thing she loved most in the world. So long as she remembered that she didn't feel so bad about her part in the subterfuge.

*****

Gallant was still sulking but at least he was over being outwardly resentful toward Jack. The trailer was ready and loaded for their trip to Greenhill Stables and Gallant was looking forward to being there again. He liked Jenny and loved the trails in that part of the country. He always secretly hoped that his friend, Marinera, would show up again one year, but he realized that probably wouldn't happen. She must be enjoying her life somewhere far away by now. He hoped she was happy and had found a job she liked as much as he loved endurance.

Jack loaded Gallant into the trailer, and they took off on the three-hour journey to Greenhill Stables. Jack had a lot to look forward to that summer, but that had all been somewhat tainted by Gracie's reunion with Gallant. He had been so excited about training hard for the Virginia City 100, a ride that began in the old mining town of Virginia City and traversed the old mining roads once used to bring supplies to the mining camps. It was a difficult ride, and he and Gallant had never attempted one hundred miles in under twenty-four hours, but they needed to know they could do it before deciding whether to attempt the Tevis Cup later that year, or to wait until the next.

Jack was also looking forward to seeing the wild mustangs that lived on the high desert plains and mountains in Northern Nevada. He was fascinated by the tales of the wild horses that scrounged out a living in such a wild and desolate part of the country, and he hoped that he might spot a few of the horses while he was there. Jenny had agreed to crew for him, and before all this happened with Gracie, he had been sure that Gallant was up to the task and would perform well. Now that girl had caused a problem with his horse, and he wasn't happy about it.

Looking back, he realized that she could have walked away before Gallant ever saw her. She could see when he came across the finish that he was well taken care of and excelling in endurance. She should have been happy knowing that, and she should have walked away. Instead, she had chosen to fawn all over him and rekindle their juvenile love affair, leaving him with a horse that was confused and restless, not knowing where his true loyalties lay. Jack was glad they were escaping to Aunt Jenny's for the summer so they would be far away from the girl and all her misguided ideas about some sort of permanent reunion. He realized now that she would only be happy if she could get Gallant all to herself once again.

And that wasn't going to happen.

*****

Gracie had arrived at Jenny's the day before and was enjoying settling in and finding out what Jenny expected of her over the summer. She couldn't help liking Jenny despite her part in separating her from Gallant, and that made her feel worse about not disclosing her true motives for being there that summer. She also realized she hadn't considered what damage her behavior might cause between Jenny and her parents. Even though her parents had played no conscious part in Gracie's plan, they could possibly lose their trainer because of her. Gracie was beginning to regret her impulsiveness to be with Gallant at any cost. Maybe if she'd thought it through, and been honest with her parents, there could have been a better way.

Jack and his father pulled up to the stables and stepped out of the truck, stretching and taking a deep breath of the clean, cool mountain air. Jack was happy to be back at what he considered his second home. It was close to lunchtime and Jenny was probably inside fixing lunch for them. Jack unloaded Gallant so he could get him settled in his pen before looking for Jenny in the main house. The horse was still acting subdued, as if he were grieving the loss of Gracie once again.

Thinking about the problem with Gracie had distracted Jack so much on the way there that he'd forgotten about Flash. As he led Gallant into the barn, there was the stallion, standing in his old pen looking at them both walking toward him. It had only been a week since the Fireworks ride and the memories there were fresh in all their minds. In a strange way, Jack was happy to see Flash at the stables, away from his owner. Maybe he could teach the horse that not all people were like Dirk—some could be trusted and depended on. On the other hand, Jack was worried about his aunt riding the stallion. He had seen firsthand how dangerous he could be. He would need to figure out what they could do to help the horse without endangering themselves.

*****

Flash could not believe his eyes. What the heck was the Upstart doing back here? This was a nightmare. He didn't think his week could get any worse, and then the Upstart showed up. Flash was fully recovered from the exertion of the Fireworks ride and had replayed all his mistakes in his mind. Gallant should never have managed to get ahead of him at the final river crossing. Flash should have anticipated his move and knocked him off his feet sooner, sending him and the boy downstream so far that he would have plenty of time to reach the finish first. Flash didn't think of that as cheating, merely strategizing for the best outcome. Next time he wouldn't be caught off guard like that. Now here was the Upstart coming to gloat about his successes and rub it in Flash's nose all summer. He wouldn't stand for it! If they rode together, he would find a way to take the Upstart out, injure him so he wouldn't even be able to start another race, let alone win one.

The boy put Gallant into his old pen next to Flash. Wonderful. Now he really wouldn't be able to escape Gallant's gloating commentary. He decided to hit where he thought it would hurt the most before Gallant had the chance to speak.

"So where is your precious girl, Gallant? I've never seen a horse look so pathetic as you did fawning all over her at the finish. How embarrassing!"

Gallant looked across at him. He was strangely quiet considering his big win last week. It was as if he had only just realized where he was.

"Flash," he said, noticing the stallion for the first time. "I meant to tell you after the race what an amazing job you did. You should have been proud of yourself. It was a close finish and if you hadn't had trouble at the river you probably would have beat me. I'm sorry your owner is such a jerk and didn't appreciate what you did that day."

Flash was thrown off guard. What? No gloating? The Upstart was weaker than he thought. He couldn't even take credit for his own win. It was pathetic.

"Are you kidding me, Upstart?" he spat out. "How condescending you are, throwing me a bone, telling me I *might* have been able to win. Of course I could have won! There were mere seconds between us. If you hadn't pulled that prank in the water and tried to drown me, I would have finished way ahead of you."

"What?" Gallant said, feeling himself come swiftly back to the present as anger started to boil in his gut. "Are you accusing me of cheating? After everything *you* did? That is too ridiculous to even justify an answer. I had a lot of respect for you at the finish of that ride, but your words have destroyed that. You truly are a mean and soulless being. I pity you, Flash." Gallant turned away, ending the conversation, but Flash would have none of it.

"I asked you about your precious little girl, Gallant. Did you cry and stomp your feet like a baby when you were taken from her again? I don't know if you'll survive the separation from her twice! You completely fell apart last time. What will you do this time? Lie down in your stall and refuse to get up like the big baby you are? Talk about no respect. I have *never* respected you. *You* are the pathetic one here."

Gallant could not help listening to Flash's cruel words, as much as he would have liked to shut them out. He wished that Flash hadn't witnessed his reunion with Gracie at the finish. He was turning something beautiful into something demeaning. He couldn't understand how Flash could be so handsome on the outside and so ugly on the inside. There was one more thing he didn't understand.

He turned his head and looked at Flash. "How would you know that Gracie and I were separated again?" he asked.

Flash looked at him with a glint in his eye. Oh, this was such sweet news to deliver. Gallant would be so caught up in his cry-baby emotions that he would never be able to focus out on the trails. His season would be over.

"I *know*, you pathetic excuse for a horse," he began, "because your precious girl is *here*."

Chapter Twenty-Six

STAND WITH EVERY OUNCE OF STRENGTH YOU HAVE LEFT

G racie had just finished setting the table for her and Jenny's lunch when Jenny heard a noise outside the front door and broke into a huge grin.

"They're here!" she said to Gracie. "Set the table for two more people, please!" Jenny went to open the front door for her guests, leaving Gracie standing alone in the kitchen. She knew who was here. It had to be him. Which meant Gallant was over there in the barn, just a few hundred feet away from where she stood. Before she could go to him, she had to face what she had done. She had to face Jack and Jenny and tell them the truth about why she was here and hope they understood her actions.

Her heart was racing. Jenny was so nice, she told herself. Surely she would understand. And Jack had been kind to her at the ride. He hadn't yelled at her or done anything that wasn't fair and honest. Maybe she was wrong to worry about their reactions. Maybe Jack would come into the kitchen and be happy to see her. They had got along well enough at the ride, hadn't they?

She wiped her sweaty palms on her jeans and, at the sound of their voices coming closer, she stepped backward until the stove blocked her retreat. The door to the kitchen opened and Jack walked in, looking behind him and laughing at something Jenny was saying. When he turned and saw Gracie, he dropped the backpack he was carrying on the floor. His face paled as he looked from Gracie to his aunt and back to Gracie again. Then his face turned red as his fists clenched by his sides.

"Is this some kind of joke, Aunt Jenny?" he asked angrily. "What the hell is *she* doing here?"

*****

The lunch was strained to say the least. The four of them sat at the table, the grown-ups trying to make polite conversation to fill the void created by the fact that Jack was refusing to speak. He stared at his plate, taking small bites out of his sandwich while his stomach screamed rejection at anything headed its way. He felt nauseous. His insides were churning as fast as his mind. He didn't understand. How did Gracie get a job here with his aunt? She must have manipulated the whole thing so she could see Gallant and try to steal him back again. He had completely misjudged her at the ride, thinking she was this sweet, honest little thing when in fact she was the complete opposite. He didn't trust himself to speak with her in the room.

Once Jenny and Jack's father, Tom, were done eating, Jenny addressed the two others.

"Jack, Gracie. I don't know exactly what is going on here, but I think I have a fair idea. I'm going to saddle up Flash and do a little arena work with him. I want the two of you to talk this out like the young adults that you are, and then when I get back, we'll all sit down together. Jack," she said, looking pointedly at her nephew. "Remember your manners. Gracie is the daughter of a very good client of mine." With that warning, the adults left.

Gracie and Jack sat there in an uncomfortable silence. After a few awkward moments Gracie spoke first, realizing that she had been unfair to spring this on him, and owed him both an explanation and an apology.

"Jack," she began, "I am so sorry. I know how this must look..."

"Do you?" Jack jumped in immediately. "Do you really know how this looks? Let me tell you, just in case you don't have a clear picture in that silly little thirteen-year-old brain of yours. It looks like you manipulated my aunt for your own gains. It looks like you are here trying to get on my good side, although you've failed dismally at that, I can assure you. It looks like you want to steal my horse, Gracie. Is that your plan? To ruin him for me because he will be so confused with you here that he won't be able to train? And then, when he can't do his job, you'll steal him from me and take him home to that place with the stupid name that you live in? The Valley of Heart's something, is it? Maybe the Valley of Dishonesty, or the Valley of Taking What You Want, regardless of how it affects others, maybe the Valley of You're a Horrible Little Girl who doesn't deserve a horse like Gallant. How about that!" Jack slammed his fist on the table, and a glass smashed to the floor into a million tiny pieces.

Right now, that was what Gracie's heart was doing. She had always tried hard to be a good person, to be nice, to be helpful. How had she turned into this person that Jack was describing? Is this who she really was underneath it all? Did she even know herself?

Her face crumpled as she pushed herself away from the table and stood up. She looked at Jack's enraged face and covering her mouth with her hand she fled. She fled from the room, from Jack's anger, from the questions and doubts she had about herself. She realized in horror what she had done to her parents. How could she have ever thought they planned the whole separation from Gallant? She knew in her heart they would never intentionally hurt her. She fled toward the barn because that was where she always went when she was upset, then realized Jenny might be in there and she couldn't face seeing her disappointment. Gracie ran around the building and saw a horse saddled and tied to the hitching post there. Riding had always been her escape, the place where she sorted out her feelings and her life, cleared her head and found her comfort. In a panicked state, she unhooked the lead rope from the bridle and threw herself into the saddle. Turning the horse toward the open gate that she knew led to the trails, she kicked him into a fast gallop.

"Yah!" she screamed. "Yah!" encouraging the horse to run faster, letting the wind wash the tears from her face, trying desperately to outrun her disgrace.

As her mind calmed, she realized she was galloping down a trail she didn't know on a horse she had never ridden, and the realization jarred her back to the present. What had she done? Now Jack could add horse thief to his list of accusations. She pulled back on the reins to slow the horse down but there was no response. She stared down at the useless reins in her hands trying to figure out what to do and noticed the deep bay coat and the powerful muscles of a horse's shoulders moving in front of the saddle, his thundering strides carrying them down the trail at breakneck speed. But it was only when she saw the black mohawk running the length of the horse's neck that Gracie realized the full extent of what she had done.

She was riding the stallion. The dangerous one. The one with no regard for human life. She was at the mercy of Gallant's archnemesis, Flash.

*****

Flash could not believe how his luck had changed. Here he was with Gallant's precious girl completely at his mercy. Her life was in his hands. He could decide whether to return her safely to the barn or dump her off a cliff. What would Gallant say if he could see him now? Flash continued to thunder along the trail, knowing exactly where he was going.

He had to give the girl credit. She was screaming less than some of the idiots who had been hired to ride him. She kept trying to pull back on his reins, but he had the bit in his teeth and nothing she did or said had any effect on him.

He felt powerful, knowing he was the one in control. He was a fit horse who could run far without getting tired. He carried Gracie farther and farther from the stables, long stretched-out strides sweeping along the trails, his satisfaction of having Gallant's most precious thing making him reckless.

As he flew around the next corner, he realized that the trail had been redirected since three years ago, and where he expected it to go right, the trail now took a sharp left. The direction he had taken was blocked by a large tree trunk laying across the trail, its stripped branches pointing like spears toward his chest.

Flash stopped as quickly as he could, but not fast enough. He felt one of the branches go deep into his chest and stay there. He heard the sound of it tearing into his flesh as the force of the collision pinned him against the trunk of the tree. Then he only heard silence.

*****

Flash did not feel the weight of the girl anymore. Where had she gone? Had she fallen or gone over his head? Flash didn't know. All he knew was that he was in serious trouble. This might have cost him his career, or, he thought, as he felt the warm trickle of blood running down the inside of his leg, it may have cost him his life.

He closed his eyes, listening for the voice that was always there in his darkest moments. "You must stand," it said. "Stay standing for as long as you can bear it."

So, despite the pain and the blood, despite the fear and the knowledge that this could be his final hours, Flash stood.

The foal he had once been watched from the bushes. *Stand*, he encouraged his older self. *Stand like we did for hours over our mother's cold body. Stand with every ounce of strength you have left, despite the life-blood pooling at your feet. You are The Almighty Flash and now, more than ever, you must live up to the name she gave us.* The foal edged closer, sniffing the sharp metallic smell that he remembered from his birth. He looked up at the horse he had become, feeling more than just the pain of his injury. He felt the pain in his heart. The loneliness of a life without love, of never feeling, or connecting. He felt the weight of the guilt he carried for the life that was sacrificed so that he could live.

I think she loved us, the foal said, wanting to offer comfort. He remembered the look in his mother's eyes as she saw him for the first and last time. It was the look of a mother grieving the loss of her son with everything she had. She hadn't wanted to go. She hadn't wanted to leave them. The impact of her love hit them both at the same time. A jolt of knowing. Despite what she had said, they knew without a doubt that she had been their mother, and she had loved them more in those last few minutes than some would ever be loved in a whole lifetime.

The foal stood taller with this knowledge, looking himself in the eye. *She's here with us now,* he said, seeing her soft brown eyes watching over them both. *For her sake, stand,* he commanded. *We survived before on will-power alone. We can do it again...*

Epilogue

RUN FREE TILL WE MEET AGAIN

"Grandma, the book can't end there!" Thomas whined.

"Why not?" Grace said, smiling down at her Grandson.

"We don't know what happens to Flash, or to Gallant, or Gracie!" Thomas was quite flustered. He wanted to know what happened next in the story.

His Papa smiled at him. "I told you it was quite the adventure, Thomas. But there are many more adventures to come. This was just the beginning!"

"I sat really still, and was good, wasn't I, Papa? So you *must* read me the next book! I'm old enough to hear *all* of it now!"

Jack nodded at his Grandson. "You really did do very well, but why don't we go for a little walk, Thomas. We all need to stretch our legs after sitting for so long. I have something to show you that I think you'll be interested in down near the stables."

Thomas loved surprises and ran quickly to the front door where he found his shoes and put them on hurriedly.

"Did we used to do things so fast all the time?" Jack asked Grace.

"I can't remember! But we were most definitely faster than we are now!" she replied, smiling. Grace got up from the couch and made her way over to the dining table where a small vase of flowers sat in the center. She plucked two beautiful flowers out of the bouquet and took them over to where Thomas was waiting by the front door.

"Can you carry these for me, Thomas?" she asked.

The three of them stepped outside. It was a beautiful summer evening. Still light, even though it was almost dinner time, the trees framed against a beautiful blue California sky. There was a very light breeze, just enough to make the trees whisper as they walked past them heading down the long driveway toward the barn.

"Look to your left, Thomas," Grace said. "Look who has finally come to visit!"

A small herd of deer had entered the grassy paddock and were munching the green shoots of grass. Their heads rose in unison when they heard the humans walking by, but they were far enough away to feel safe and soon dropped their heads to resume their grazing.

When they got close to the stables, Grace turned off the driveway to a path that led to a bench where the view over the treetops stretched for miles. Thomas had never known this bench was here.

"This is where Gallant is laid to rest, Thomas," Grace said.

"Papa made me this bench so that I could sit and be with him any time I feel like it."

The bench had an inscription that read, "Here lies Gallant, my first love. Run free till we meet again."

Thomas felt the importance of this sacred spot now that he knew who the occupant was.

Grace looked at her Grandson. "Can you lay one of the flowers down for him, Thomas? I always feel like I'm blowing him a kiss when I do that. I imagine him running across the fields of heaven, the wind lifting his mane, and when he feels my kiss on the breeze, he whinnies to me, just like he did when I was a child."

Jack reached for his wife's hand, knowing that even after all these years her heart still ached for her friend.

Thomas solemnly laid the flower down next to the bench and thought of the horse that lay there.

"He was so fast and so brave, wasn't he Grandma!" he said. Grace nodded her head.

"Who's the other flower for, Papa?" Thomas asked, curious as to why they had brought two.

"Why don't you come with me and I'll show you, Thomas," Jack said. "Let's leave Grandma alone with Gallant for a moment."

Jack took Thomas by the hand and they went to another spot about thirty feet away, partially hidden by the trees. If you didn't know it was there you might have missed it entirely. There was a shiny bronze plaque mounted on a small concrete monument, the grass neatly trimmed back to keep the area clear. Thomas walked over to the plaque and began reading.

"Here lies The Almighty Flash..." He turned his head in surprise to his grandfather.

"Flash is here? Why?" he queried.

"Just read on, Thomas," Jack said.

"Here lies The Almighty Flash. A magnificent warrior. A loyal friend. Sire of the famous Redemption. Wow, Papa! How did Flash go from being so mean and scary to that?"

Jack laughed. "Well, that is another wonderful story. As you learn more about Gallant and your grandmother, you will also find that under the right circumstances, and given a chance, even a horse with a soul as dark as The Almighty Flash has a chance to redeem himself." Thomas stood there in awe, wondering how that would ever happen. The man and boy, generations apart, stood together, each thinking of a horse that could have been destroyed had fate not stepped in and guided him in another direction.

Gracie sat on the bench overlooking the pastures and enjoying the sight of the ocean in the distance as it blended into the horizon. Even though everything in the book had happened so long ago she could still imagine it like it was yesterday. She had cried into many a horse's mane since Gallant had gone. She had ridden thousands of miles with so many wonderful horses beneath her, and yet he would always be her first love, just like the inscription on the bench said.

She breathed deeply. One day she knew they would be together again. She knew that just beyond the space she could see, and the world she could touch, he was waiting for her. His magnificent face looking for her always, ears forward, just as he had from his stall in the Valley of Heart's Delight when he was a foal. Somewhere he was running up and down an invisible fence line waiting for her school bus to drop her at the end of the driveway, and he would hear her footsteps and her sweet voice humming a tune as she walked toward him, her backpack bouncing behind her, lunchbox swinging by her side.

And one day, not too far in the future, as he listens for her voice on the wind, he will finally hear her calling to him, and he will run to her side full of joy to see his girl again, dropping his head once more into her arms, and she will cry with joy into his mane. Once again, and forever, she will be with her first love.

Her Gallant. *Always*.

THE END

Acknowledgements

This book would not have been written at all without the inspiration of my dear friend, Julie Suhr. She loaned me some of her childhood memories and her beautiful horse, HCC Gazal, who became my Gallant. Without her I doubt I would have written this book at all.

I would like to thank my husband, Troy, and all my family for their support during this project.

Phylicia Mann enthusiastically joined the project, and her beautiful illustrations and cover artwork brought my characters to life. She is one talented lady! Check out some of her other projects at www.pmannsculpture.com.

A huge nod of thanks goes to my editor, Carmen Smith, who put me through editing bootcamp with just the right amount of constructive criticism and encouragement. I cannot thank her enough for all she contributed to this project.

To my team at Mill City Press, thank you all for your patience and hard work.

Foreword Publicity, led by Alysson Bourque and Lori Orlinsky, are the best marketing and publicity team out there. Thank you for all you do. A book is silent unless it is read. Thank you for giving my books a loud voice.

Mandy Holland, DVM agreed to be my veterinary resource for the series, and I plan on getting my money's worth out of her. She may not have known exactly what she signed up for.

For proofreading the manuscript (multiple times!) I would like to thank Julie Suhr and also my stepmother, Hazel Fuller. Also thank you to Riley Rood for being such a great junior proofreader. Your comments ended up in me adding Part Three to the book!

I was also inspired by our incredible endurance community where I have found so many friendships and so much support. A huge shout out to the ride managers, who work relentlessly and without nearly enough recognition, and without whom these rides and this sport would not exist.

Thank you to all the horses who have given all they had to this sport. They are the athletes that allow us to follow our dreams.

Huge apologies to our wonderful RMC Flash Gordon (The Almighty Flash). You make a terrific badass in these books, but I know you have a heart of gold. You showed us what a horse with an indominable spirit is capable of, and it was more than we could have ever imagined. You will be well cared for until the end of your days.

And lastly, thank you to my readers. I hope you fell in love with my characters as much as I did, and that this book inspires you all to hear The Call of The Trail!!!

Claire Eckard, July 2021

List of Resources

www.aerc.org
American Endurance Ride Conference

www.teviscup.org
Official site/ All things Tevis

www.irunfar.com
Ultra running site/Western States 100

www.wdra.net
Western Distance Riders Alliance

www.equinedistanceriding.com
EDRA

www.natrc.org
North American Trail Conference

www.rideandtie.org
Ride and Tie

www.facebook.com/wstmuseum
Western States Museum Facebook

www.westernstatestrailmuseum.org
Western States Museum Website

https://sccha.wildapricot.org
Fireworks Endurance Rides

www.thelongridersguild.com
Expedition Journal and Bookstore

www.pmannsculpture.com
Phylicia Mann Artist Webpage

www.claireeckardauthor.com
Claire Eckard Author Website

GALLANT

The Call of the Mustangs

Fall 2022

**Do not miss the special feature on the next page –
A poem/song written by the author,
The Last Battle Cry.**

The Last Battle Cry, by Claire Eckard

To the horses who make us, who shape us and break us
The lessons they teach us will never be taught
'Till we climb in the saddle, put feet in the stirrups
And say 'let us ride in the name of this sport'

To the horses who carry us, knowing God willing
We'll bring them back safe, once the journey is done
The call of the trail is as loud as the thunder
And all those who finish will know they have won.

And we'll tell the story, of how you were gallant
And how you found heaven in thundering skies
We'll cry at our losses and weep for the horses
Who gave all they had till the last battle cry.

To the horses who carry us through the deep canyons
Who risk all they have in the quest for our fame,
Who travel in darkness and brave every shadow,
We promise to always remember your name

To the horses who loved us and chose to be with us
When green fields were calling, and friends were nearby,
We thank you for making our dreams last forever
We'll never forget you were here by our side.

And we'll tell the story, of how you were gallant
And how you found heaven in thundering skies
We'll cry at our losses and weep for the horses
Who gave all they had till the last battle cry.

We'll weave pretty flowers into your long mane, as you
lay in the grave we have made for you here.
We'll steal from your tail for a memory braid, which
We'll wrap 'round our wrist so you'll always be near.

To the horses who lay here in this hallowed ground
The lessons they taught us we won't soon forget
Through the pain of goodbye, we will smile at
your memory.
For horses we've loved there will be no regrets

And we'll tell the story, of how you were gallant
And how you found heaven in thundering skies
We'll cry at our losses and weep for the horses
Who gave all they had till the last battle cry.